THE SAGES OF WEST 47TH STREET

and Other Tales of Becoming

THE SAGES OF WEST 47TH STREET

and Other Tales of Becoming

J.L. COOPER

Carmichael, CA / 2018

Table of Contents

Dedication

To my family and every friend I've ever had. To our follies and triumphs, and all our serious silences.

Introduction

These memoirs and creative nonfiction stories tell mostly of my youth and early twenties, the psychologist in the boy, childhood in a suburban town during the Cold War followed by a willful outward push into the world, taking to the road. Memories are ephemeral, with shadows and streaks of light breaking through. I've found great richness in relationships, as well as in private thought. In the stillness of remembering, important people from my past return with surprising ease. The later pieces are reflective vignettes, following a muse who refuses any interest in linear time. Regardless of the age of characters, everyone is in the making. Many of the characters in these stories are disguised in name and identifying details.

Acknowledgments

I'm grateful to the editors of the following journals where pieces
in this collection were first published.

"Wood Swivel Chairs:
Second Place Essay
Literal Latte, 2014

"A Summoning of Gifts to Wet Ankles"
First Prize, Short Short Story Contest
New Millennium Writings, 2013

"The Sages of West 47th Street"
First Runner-up, Nonfiction Contest, 2016. Judge: Meghan Daum
StoryQuarterly, Vol. 50
Featured at *Sacramento Stories on Stage*: August 25, 2017
Read by Actor: Eric Baldwin

"The Annunciation of Charles Nightcloud"
Gold Man Review, Issue 5, 2016

"The Four Corners of the World"
Sisyphus, Issue 4.4, 2017/18

"Inheritance"
Hippocampus Magazine
April 1, 2016

"Willing Branches"
Getting Old: An Anthology
KY Story, 2015

"In Case of Rapture"
Kentucky Review, 2015

"Foggy Day at Heisler Park"
Here Comes The Sun: Beach Reads
Third Street Writers, Laguna Beach, 2017

Wood Swivel Chairs

In 1959 I was a nine-year-old freckled blond kid wearing a Red Sox little league hat just to the left of center, hungry for swings at wild pitches and the chase of impossible fly balls. On Saturdays after games, my father brought me to the newsroom where he worked as city desk editor for a small paper struggling to remain a daily. He'd sit in an oak swivel chair with no pad on it, among six other desks belonging to his reporters. He'd put his legs up on the heavy desk, with no bend in the knees, and cross his ankles so that the sole of the right shoe took the full weight of both legs. I'd sit in one of the chairs next to him and spin around in various angles of tilt while he finished his writing or editing. When he was working on something potent, his whole body would freeze while clutching his coffee cup three inches above the desk, until something clicked in his mind. The building could have been on fire and he wouldn't move until the click. He wouldn't file confusion away for later pondering. Soon enough, he'd come back into fluid motion, but something of that sequence lives oddly in me as both reassuring and puzzling, as thunder on the horizon or a dream where I'm not me.

It's odd to have learned both patience and impatience from the same father. At nine, I'd be standing in the batter's box, waiting for a pitch, and sometimes the pitcher was in a kind of trance, doing his ritual or trying to read my stance. I knew the pitch would come, but not how or when. It was a little like watching my dad edit, where his alertness was seduced by a mix of wills, producing a great curiosity. In another twenty years, I'd be telling my father about wanting to be a psychologist, but the original scene from the spinning chairs was the template: a scene punctuated by jars of glue, various sizes of scissors, and graphite pencils as dull as the edge of night. He'd circle words and phrases in the flash of an old-style filament photo bulb, plowing through a pile of copy with all manner of artful symbols. Then he'd cut and paste with lightning speed. For half the stories he wrote, he doubled as photographer, taking photos for news and feature stories using his beloved Graflex 4x5, with its cool bellows. When he came back from the field he'd have film plates stuffed in every jacket pocket. Someone stole the camera, but not its trace in me.

I loved to follow him as he dropped film plates off in the darkroom: a room enticing far beyond its name. All the mysterious odors, metal trays, and safe lights produced a muffled magical world. It took two minutes to adjust my eyes to the special light; some things can't be hurried. I made sure I had a darkroom of my own for the next thirty years, owing to the fact he taught me how to see the positive image in the drying negative. He'd talk of potential space and how he'd crop the photo for maximum emphasis, then show me how to dodge and burn the image using his hand to control the light from the enlarger. He was concrete where I was given to metaphor. He invited me to look for the story of a person in grey tones under a safe light. This came to me when skipping a stone in my forties. The stone went under, as all do, but why did it take so long to recognize what else he was trying to get me to be curious about? Back in the 1950's, my father soon transitioned from the Graflex to a twin lens Rolleiflex. Journalism was changing. I remember him loving that camera too.

He said, "Some stories need photos, and some photos are ruined with words."

I asked, "What do you mean?"

"Different ways of telling," was his reassurance, adding, "It took me a long time."

And typewriters: my God he knew their ways. When he died last year I found all five he used in his career. I gave one heavy monster away, along with a temperamental portable he once threw off a balcony. I kept the Royal typewriters because they still speak to me about him. They push back, demand you mean something, and insist on a heavy intention. The carriage return requires a visceral appreciation of line breaks. His world thumped along in chunks of advancing paper.

When he'd pull a piece of paper out of his Royal, it was definitive; the roller would spin a few extra rounds. I was far from definitive when I told him at twenty-nine I wanted to be a psychologist. I knew he did not trust silence in the newsroom, and he did not trust psychologists for their seeming obscurity, although he'd never been to one. He appreciated a different kind of action: a major story breaking over the newswire. When that happened, everyone rushed from their desks to huddle in front of the machine. Nobody dared speak. The machine would vibrate and even rock if the key strikes were rhythmic enough. It was a crisis if it ran out of paper when something big was coming in. His favorite greeting when answering his phone was, "Give it to me in a punchy nutshell." I remember his initial distrust of light touches in electric typewriters.

By 1979, I'd been receiving clinical supervision from a man in his seventies, who taught me that the quality of silence is at least half of what you work with in psychotherapy. He called silence a privilege and a curse, sometimes a refuge, or pure creative space, refusing to clarify. He said if you cure the madness of needing to cure something, value is found in nuance and self-observation. He said a hundred things like that, telling me how progress requires immersion, suspension of conclusion, appreciation of differences. Also the well-timed observation, the acceptance of bottomless gulfs and the bridges yet sought.

Here's the setting for me telling my father about my career choice; we're in the family room. I've got long hair in a ponytail. He's got a crew cut like when he was still in the Marines. This was going to be a hard sell to an ex-marine Lt. Colonel and a journalist. His every instinct was to get the story and move on to the next. He was also a master of unexpected comments my whole life, this time saying, "Look over there in the bookshelf: The Harvard Classics and my personal favorites, Rudyard Kipling and Robert Service. Give me an Irish song. I've memorized dozens of poems on the great themes of being alive just because they moved me. But in my generation nobody told me what a psychologist does. When I was growing up people didn't go to them unless they needed to be in the hospital or were rich and could afford psychoanalysis. Analysts back then were loathe to speak to journalists, like we were going to reduce what they said into something stupid, but actually that's what they thought of us, and seemingly—the rest of the world. What got me was the bastards didn't even try to explain what they did. It's like they guarded a secret world and I had the impression they wouldn't even tell their patients what they were trying to do. In my world, you interview someone and get to the point, and you don't put up with evasive answers. The story either makes the news

or gets killed, or gets the shit edited out of it. I got to a point where I'd rather see my stories get killed than edited, so my solution was to become an editor. Then the bad thing didn't happen so much."

While hearing his words, I regressed to feeling nine again, to the mix of excitement and fear when he'd take me to the room where lead chunks from Linotype machines were melted down in a giant open cylinder to be recycled for the next edition. The furnace was always burning. He'd lift me up seven feet in the air to look down and see the melting words for myself. Every single man working a Linotype machine was a chain smoker, filling his lungs with unfiltered cigarettes, carbon dust and the stench of melted lead. They loved the sweaty action as much as I've ever seen anyone love their work. The machines were as magnificent as the men running them. Everything was clicking and roaring towards deadlines. Everything was urgent. I remember the day when my father paused and spoke, over the din of pre-electric typewriters, "The fate of words is hot lead, unless you remember the words yourself."

I asked him, "How will I know which words to remember?" He smiled, but wouldn't linger, saying, "You'll know. You'll feel a pull that won't let go," then he'd be off to seeing how one of his reporters was doing. When he came back to his desk, I'd be spinning again, doodling with one of his graphite pencils, wondering about unknowable things. It remains a mystery how I suddenly remembered the melting words, then came back to the moment in the family room to hear him say, "So you want to be a psychologist. Can you explain what a psychologist does in a punchy nutshell?"

I said it wouldn't be so easy to talk about psychotherapy like it could be explained in a punchy nutshell. But he had a fundamental distrust of lengthy reasoning, and persisted in this vein because that was the vein he knew. Here comes his impatient side. He set the stage, saying, "OK, my father sold cosmetics. My own father

Linotypes working the hot lead

didn't believe in the value of college so he didn't pay for it or show up at my graduation. Otherwise he didn't oppose my going. That's the deal I got. Grudgingly, he became proud of me, or if he was proud all along, I was the last to know. His father was a foreman in a coal mine. Son of a bitch to work for, I'm told. Our ancestors came from Ireland and Wales. I'm here because I didn't get shot down when I was a pilot in two wars. My best friend was killed in WWII. I love your mother, you, and your sister, and I love journalism, every part of it except selling classified ads. Punchy Nutshell. Now, what about you?"

It's easy for an enthusiastic young man to feel doomed right when he wants his father to appreciate something he has to say. But knowing a bit of his language, I said, "I try to help people make sense of the lives they find themselves living, and when they step out of a script they feel trapped in, I'm both catalyst and witness, but never in ways I'm fully aware of. I try to figure out the template of how someone uses the word 'I,' but it's not like a dentist who fixes a tooth and everybody is happy. I love every bit of it so far, except the prospect of working with insurance companies." He perked up, but I could see he was skeptical by his lowered tone, plus he hated passive references.

I kept on. "You know how the human psyche likes simple explanations on one level, but doesn't trust them on another? I get people to elaborate, to tell their story. It's incredible to think everyone is telling an amazing story without even knowing it. Somewhere in there, my way of listening becomes part of the mix, and the plot has legs that carry a theme forward, like a good newspaper story. There is no tidy resolution." He asked, "Is this like rats going through the maze quicker to find the cheese?" I said, bluntly, "No."

I was looking for common ground, irritated and losing steam. He said, "Sometimes I get a story from a reporter and he makes an interesting story look as dull as gum on the bottom of your shoe. I'm not so good fixing that. How do you help someone who doesn't believe life is even interesting?"

"Psychologists get desperate just like journalists. We lose the thread, look in the wrong places, miss the clues, and get stuck in the wish for a different plot. The story of a life is not told willingly. I try not to get bogged down in anyone's bitterness, anger, depression. I don't much trust a summary. I've read too many medical notes that don't capture anything meaningful about a person. I love it when someone finds a way to describe things that are impossible to know. That's art, and that's why psychotherapy is not about giving answers and going home with a warm feeling."

None of this took flight with him. Way too abstract.

I stood there remembering the first thing he did before writing or editing was to sweep aside the mess of yesterday's stories to the newsroom floor. He'd set his broad elbow down, open the palm of his hand and sweep every piece of paper off his desk. There wasn't one hint of anger in this motion. It was a deliberate, meditative cleansing: a moment of centering. After clearing his desk he'd sit quietly for a maximum of one minute before orienting himself to the sounds of the teletype machine and the ringing of phones. Then he'd gather yesterday's papers from the floor and chuck it all to a wide-rimmed can. I never discovered where he learned this trick of living, since his father warned him constantly to live in anticipation of an insecure world, plus never to throw anything away.

Maybe it's really that simple, he didn't want to be much like his father. I wanted to pick and choose traits I admired from both parents, but of course it never works that way. Not in the slightest. As a family, we were huge fans of the original *Twilight Zone* series on TV, and the plot twists pointed toward our fondness for unexpected endings. My father was fond of saying the trick was to figure out why a story needs to be told. My sister and I learned we had permission to create a story worthy of its ending, as much of life is bracing for the twist at the end. It was my mother who knew this intuitively. She was the wise one, remote too, always seeing more than I knew.

When I turned twenty, the Vietnam War had escalated beyond belief. It seemed like it wouldn't end, and worse, it was tearing families apart with ease. The nation too. Looking back, I had a bit of envy for my father's generation. All the phases of his journalism career, the general life plan after WWII, the sense of right, unfolded like the elegant movements of a Brahms symphony for him. But my life was feeling more like Stravinsky's Firebird Suite.

A train comes off the tracks going too fast around a curve, and ours was already tilting. Provocation touches the edges of things generational, refusing to be named. I told him how I came to love good stories because of his way of telling, in first person, in unexpected ways. I added, "You know, good people evade stuff all the time, leave out the main part, mostly without knowing it. Everybody edits their own story, or sometimes kill it themselves. That's my world as a psychologist much as anything else." Then he got upset, and I felt the cauldron of hot lead separating us.

He said, "What do you mean by those words? People don't kill their own stories? Why would they?" I was reminded of his uncanny way of staying at the cutting edge of his own life. He was the opposite of an anxious guy. My father pondered great questions when pruning his grapefruit tree, but kept any hint of personal doubt from me. "All right," he said, "Maybe we're talking about what's important to get at. There's an art to a brief interview. I might have one minute with a person in the news. It doesn't matter if they just won the Nobel Prize or a Pulitzer, got elected Senator, or witnessed a warehouse fire. I go to their turf, their laboratory, the capitol, a street corner, and make it my business to draw them out. The camera and the notepad come out, and I'll ask them to say what they did or were trying to do. Jonas Salk got right down to it, telling me in an interview, 'I found a way to prevent polio.' That's how an interview should go. I loved it. The best people are always direct. The details are fillers. Armand Hammer was sitting with Dr. Salk at the time, and handed him a check for a million dollars to support his research. That was a lot of money in those days. He said something like, 'I want to support this great cause.' See, straight to the point. I talked to Walt Disney when he was planning Disneyland. He told me he wanted to fill the space of an orange grove with a dream he had in his mind, and that's just what he did. James Cash Penney shook my hand in a way I'll never forget, formal and gracious at the same time. Impeccably dressed man. He wanted to upgrade the common man, and he did when he ran J.C. Penney. Boom, he stated his credo. I don't forget the essence of a person even if I just have a one-minute interview. A lot of people don't do the thing they want to accomplish, but my part is to ask something vital, to get it out in the open. Now tell me again about psychotherapy."

I was closer to my father's mind than ever. There was no going back, so I told my piece as best I could.

"In my world, you draw out that exact thought, carrying something in the open as far as you can, but it's the other person who needs to hear themselves the most. I have this idea that tension can be held by two people and good things can come from it, but I don't get to know for quite a while what form it will take or what I must witness before anything meaningful gets said. Often the tension ruptures, resisting any form at all. When things go well, awareness is expanded, made safe, and a person is free to explore again. Nobody becomes a different person, but the different version is what I'm curious about. Numb compulsion no longer runs the show. There is meaning and direction where there used to be dull complaints."

But I lost him again, and suddenly realized that talking to fathers in grad school language should be outlawed, like smoking was finally banned in restaurants. I was too full of theory, brimming with thoughts of changing the world, like he once did, so I refused to apologize for passion. He declared,

"What the hell kinds of concepts are those?"

And I countered, "Let's say you don't have just a minute, and no camera is exposing this for the world to see. Let's say you have done a decent job of neutralizing shame and anxiety and other qualities that stifle a human voice, and you can hear directly from the person trying to express something really difficult. They may not even know what they're struggling with at first. I keep an ear out for that part. You showed me what to look for in negatives in the darkroom. That's what I'm doing. I'm not going to fix the root causes of emotional suffering. By the way, I've been wondering, what else did you want to ask Richard Nixon when you interviewed him early in his political career?"

He liked the question. "A lot, I wanted to know a hell of a lot, like what he was thinking between words. He was a brilliant man, regardless of what became of him. He took wrong turns, sure. I wanted to know whether he was one step ahead of questions, whether he was shy or suspicious of double meanings, but I had to be direct. A journalist doesn't ask, 'How are you doing?' A journalist asks, 'What's your stand on Proposition so-and-so?' I don't think I'd be a psychologist." At this point he was conducting the air with his hands, using his resonant speaking voice.

"The thing about news reporting is to realize you are not writing for the editorial page at that moment. The ethic is an attempt to be objective, even if there is no such thing."

Hearing this was the equivalent to finding a bridge. "I have the same deal. Nobody is objective, especially therapists, but if I look at myself, the impulses and the way I lean into a life story or away from it, and what that evokes in me, it helps me stay present and bring out some unexpected key to the story. I wonder what your life as a journalist would have been like without the different phases, like if you had stayed on as a reporter in a small town in western Nebraska and that was all she wrote?" He looked at his bookshelf, "Why in God's heaven would I want to know that hypothetical thing? I've done what made sense." He was bitter for about five seconds, OK, more like ten, OK, close to fuming, but I told him I was in awe of his answer, and it broke another logjam.

He wasn't given to speculation, so he didn't try to respond further. Then it came to me, "In my work, I'm asking about the parts that aren't for the camera. I get to meet the person without the exposure of flash bulbs." Then he told me about the time he took Psych 101 in college. They were talking about experiments with rats in overcrowded cages. He said some rats started behaving in a bizarre manner, eating each other and all, and the researchers extrapolated to humans in metropolitan areas, crime rates, etc., using ideas that didn't call for a degree in anything other than common sense. It turned him off because he was well aware of bizarre human behavior in rural parts, where there was no crowding problem to explain a damn thing. That spelled the end of his interest in psychological explanations, tipping him even more toward storytelling in journalism. He was a fine creative writer too. I searched for him in me and equally for myself in him. None of it came easily. Too close, I suppose.

Taking a step back, mid-sentence, a breeze came into the family room, blowing past the futile things I was tempted to say. I stopped arguing and was able to appreciate he was simply telling his truth, and could see him in his grand pause, as a man given to profound moments of recognition. To him, the coming of a thought was pure drama.

He looked with immense curiosity toward the future, almost daring it to reveal its intentions. He'd freeze in the middle of a forward step, loving the dramatic energy concentrated in gazes he summoned. He had the rare skill of finding a Shakespearian theme within a boring City Council meeting. He'd elevate the characters he interviewed so they would have to say something unexpected, or reveal a motive they had hidden even from themselves. People being interviewed by him had no choice but to offer some nuance of unexpected personal truth. He wouldn't pounce or gloat. He'd be humble, defer to the thing he found as being some version of truth or nonsense, but was never a friend of in-between. He'd summarize his interview in a context that forced human striving into a humanitarian quest.

After his work day, he'd come home and recite one of the poems he memorized. I learned to tell his mood by the ones he chose, whether he recited it with a twinkle or a tear. I got flashes of him being a reluctant psychologist, holding a flood of need at bay. I saw his father in him, distrusting to the end, and the father before him, who worked the coal mines of Pennsylvania and supported eight children.

The larger picture allowed me to pick up the thread, or it might be more accurate to say I made one because I needed one.

"In anthropology I learned about cultures in the South Pacific where they practiced cannibalism even though there was plenty of food and water for everybody. European diseases and imported religions weren't even part of the equation yet. I'm still wondering about that. I agree with you that not much is explained in college."

Our talk narrowed to the land of credos. He liked summaries, things you could say in a sentence.

"I like deadlines."

"I like mysteries," I replied.

When full sentences seemed unimportant, we shared a whiskey, toasting the fact we could talk and it didn't need to go anywhere in particular. But he still wanted more. A journalist always wants more.

A memory came over me like fog drifting over a redwood grove.

"Do you remember the story you covered when a whole family died on Christmas Eve of carbon monoxide poisoning? The gifts were under the lighted tree and everyone was tucked in bed on a freezing night. They tried heating the house with the stove burner, but nobody cracked a window. You told me how the firefighters came on the scene and found everyone in their beds in a state of unbelievable peace, like they would wake up and have their Christmas, but they were all gone. You told me privately how the seasoned, gruff firefighters realized there was nothing for them to do, so they came outside, collapsed in their heavy suits on the lawn, and wept. You told me when the seasoned, gruff reporters came on the scene they were so disturbed witnessing the firefighters they froze as they were getting out of their cars. Out of respect, no journalist mentioned the anguish of the firefighters in their stories. Nobody could pull their cameras to their eyes to include the firefighters, who were first witnesses to the tragedy. Somebody whispered about the family inside, but it was the scene on the lawn that haunted the reporters, and extended to everyone they told. A reporter took a picture of the front of the house, with a meaning only he would know. The story was somehow stupidly reduced to the dangers of carbon monoxide poisoning. But the image on the lawn rippled to paperboys, bartenders, families, and me. Something pissed you off in ways you couldn't talk about. I remember the day you couldn't talk. I was about twelve. It's strange how I can't even remember whether you were one of the reporters that day, the photographer, or an editor. Maybe you were all three, as you used to do it all back then. It was one of those rare times when you spoke in the third person. That's one thing I remember clearly. That's the kind of conundrum psychologists try to unravel; the aftermath, the carrying of unspeakable burden, the re-enactments large and unseen. Dad, I'm the first to admit, our tools are as dull as the edge of night."

He said he remembered the story, and hundreds like it, and was able to settle one piece of it, saying he tried to write the human tragedy part, and he wanted it to be about the firefighters as much as the family. An editor killed his story for unknown reasons, and for once I got him to speculate about himself. He thought that's probably why he was angry, that his story was killed. He wanted to interview the firefighters, but they weren't talking, and the clock was running on the deadline. Then I asked him if he was the editor, and he offered the highest honesty I have known, saying he was pretty sure it wasn't him; that some things you can tell about, but can't really write about. Or sometimes it's the other way around. Then he paused, couldn't cut and paste the exact sequence of events of that day. Too much was going on. It was a long time ago. Everyone withdrew from each other in the newsroom, upset about how the story should be told. The deadline passed. It just flat out passed, and the carbon monoxide story ran.

He collected himself in the space of two breaths and a single gulp of whisky, telling me he always intended to shield his family from the things that upset him, wars and local murders being prominent in his mind. Then, I had the rare privilege of reassuring him, saying that being a psychologist or a journalist earns you zero immunity. We choose these ways. No fatherly answer came, just two guys talking. I came his way about the pitfalls of lengthy reasoning, and then we lifted our glasses to the firefighters, and the mystery of where stories go in us. We looked over at his corner desk at exactly the same moment. Sure enough, there was his wood swivel chair from his newsroom days: always our best witness.

We kept the chair in the family for three decades after our talk. It broke one day in a dangerous way, most likely due to the cumulative effect of my spinning combined with his using it to lean back so far. I blocked the memory of who was sitting in it when it broke. I don't want to know. I don't want a psychologist to help me remember. I prefer to remember the way my father summarized our conversation in the family room, in a punchy nutshell of course, saying he wanted to hear from me what I wanted to do with my life, adding he had a rough time telling his own father what he wanted to do, and he wasn't sure why.

He just left the newsroom, so to speak, at the age of 91. His name was Jim. I'll have another drink to him and his era, when a newspaper went to bed properly, and the reporters all left at the same time, headed for bars or families. The floor was full of scraps and a fan was left on with a rhythmic clicking sound, its breeze rustling a blank yellow notepad. The words from yesterday were melted and ready for morning. That is all. That is all.

The Annunciation of Charles Nightcloud

A checkered-shirted, pockmarked angel of a trucker dropped me off ten miles outside of Socorro, New Mexico, back when I was open-ended, hitchhiking, preferring a freezing night in the high desert to an indifferent girl in Albuquerque. I walked a little further under soft white clouds. When they vanished in a moonless night, I named emerging stars. The first was Panacea, then her sister, Mirage, and cousin Sofia, which created a triangle in the southern sky with Silhouette and the red star, Mercy.

Frost framed my wool cap while thousands of stars brought certainty to my smallness. I hoped for invisibility in my sleeping bag, but a pack of coyotes caught my scent. I was a green city kid with a wild imagination, shuddering at their yelps, imagining the alpha coyote taking a lunge at my leg. The coyotes animated, making sounds too close to frenzy. I breathed again when a closer yelp quieted the pack with a definitive call. The quiet screamed back that I was a shallow breath, nothing more than the click of a breaking twig.

I remember morning. Delirium was the price for its arrival. I shook off visions of a desert death like I used to shake water from my hair after a predawn swim. When the sun cracked the desert open, it gave birth to small stark shadows. I sat on the edge of the empty road; nothing came for hours. I tossed pebbles to the pavement. Before they bounced and settled, I tried to predict the side that would face the sky, and see if being right made a difference. I was just short of naming my favorite rocks when a man walked right out of the sagebrush.

"I'm Charlie," he said, as if I'd known him in another form and needed a little hint. He'd been out there all night too. "Bitch of a night," he said, this being the first frost of the year, and he ought to know, telling me he was native to these parts and used another language when he talked to coyotes. He was the one who called the pack away from us last night. Charlie said talking to animals came easy. His real trouble was telling his wife about the bothering. He couldn't name it otherwise, but admitted she deserved to know when he was troubled and needed to come out here.

"Shall I call you Charlie?"

"Well, I'm Charlie to everyone who knows me; Sagebrush Charlie to some. I was named after my father, a man passing through. His name was Charles. Nobody knew him much, especially my mother. She taught me to talk to animals."

He looked over my shoulder, but his eyes didn't focus anywhere. "I don't know why she gave me his name. She must have seen something in him worth looking at in me. I tried asking her when she was dying, and I try asking her now, but the wind changes direction every time I think I hear her answering."

He told me he was acquainted with ditches, and said it in a noble way, like he was offering wisdom to a loved one. His habit was to stand in the road and put a thumb in the direction the next car or truck was headed.

"It doesn't matter where they're headed, since I always come back here," he said. He never ventured more than a hundred miles before turning back. He talked to men, always men, about any-thing they wanted to say—like where they wanted to go if they live long enough to retire, if they were in some pain, or what they hoped to leave or find. Soon enough, they'd show him if they pre-ferred conversation, the radio, or the wind coming through the open window. He was more at ease with wind because he likened it to a dream. Sometimes, he'd simply say, "That's far enough for me," to summarize the day. His black hair seemed in motion even when the wind abated; it covered half the worry lines in his brow—more like rivers, but not as deep as his desert eyes when they fixed on the sight of me. I was thinking he might be a Sephardic mystic, show-ing up every hundred years, or just a man overdue for recognition, maybe Sainthood, but he wasn't a man of cloth.

After all, he talked to coyotes, snakes, and birds. He was ami-able, with no judgment meant to harm. Wasn't he a variation of St. Francis? He blessed the high desert, said he was close to the source of his bothering, and it scared him less and less. He told me he was forty but knew he looked sixty. He could have been six hundred; I could see the part of him that lived beyond wind and drink.

Charlie turned in a minimal way, and asked me, dead serious, as if we were debating scriptures, what I thought would come upon us next: a pickup truck, a sedan, or an eighteen-wheeler? For the sake of shadows shortening, I asked,

"Are those my only choices?" When I saw he wasn't going to answer, I told him a white pickup will likely come next, with two men going to work.

"Is that all you've got? What else happens?"

I gave the matter my best thought, since Charlie wouldn't budge an inch from serious.

"OK, here's what happens. One of them had a big fight with his wife the night before and wants to talk about it, but can't find a way to start, so he runs his hand down his leg with tense, uncertain aim, and this gets the attention of the other man, who says, 'hey, I get those cramps too,' but the first man says, 'it's not a cramp, it's something else,' and that starts a conversation about long straight roads in deserts—how hypnotic they are. Each man takes a drink of water, but it doesn't help the other kind of thirst. Neither takes his eyes off the road while talking about their boss, who gives them constant trouble. They don't see the futility of complaining. Then the first man mentions his wife in a lowered tone, as if she's looking at him from the dashboard, trying to believe in him, but he doesn't tell about the argument, not yet, which was bruising and unfinished. He realizes she's been trying to get through to him. The wind coming in the open window flips their empty paper coffee cups around the cab of the truck. As they tumble around, each man offers a list of physical injuries he's endured. Back and forth it goes, for the next thirty miles. The good part is they both recognize a kind of sweetness on the topic of endurance."

Charlie said, "Not bad, I see a lot of that between men. A whole lot of it."

A pause came upon Charlie like a breathless visitation; he even closed his eyes. A pause in the desert is unlike any other, on account of the crusted earth and sand absorbing most of your presence and half your intention. You have to work extra hard to see what's in your mind before claiming it belongs to you, and even then, maybe it doesn't.

Charlie was at peace with that kind of uncertainty. It gave him a private smile. He took a breath as long as a cactus shadow at sundown.

"I see the men in the truck too. Although they don't like their work, they never look for other jobs. When they run dry talking about it, one man says: 'You know, we pass this stretch of road

going seventy every single day, and never stop to see what it feels like when we're not headed somewhere.' The other man says, 'Why the hell would you want to stop in the middle of nowhere,' and the first man says, 'I'm not so sure this is nowhere. What if this is where we might find a little peace but we don't stop because we're afraid to be alone and don't even know that silence can be a good thing?' The second man goes him one more, saying, 'What if it's not silence we fear, it's our insignificance?'"

Charlie was so deep in the story, and I the listening, we waited out the sound of a jet overhead because we needed the desert in our minds. He took a gentle breath.

"Well, the first man gets pissed, saying, 'you're full of shit, go ahead, stop the truck right now and we'll see, I have to piss anyway.' But they end up driving five more miles without either one speaking; each man is trying to figure out what else he means to say. The driver is uneasy, grows into his own resolve, and says, 'OK, I'm stopping now. I'm going to spend a few minutes standing out here without talking. Nothing personal. You know, you've been my best friend for twenty-seven years, I just did the numbers.'

'What do you mean, the numbers? Of course you're my best friend. I practically had to push you on the dance floor with a bulldozer when you met your wife. That's the serious fear I'm talking about. You took it from there just fine. I want a little credit. You never thanked me for getting you past your fear.'"

Charlie squared himself to me at that juncture.

"That's it, that's as far as I've gone with the imaginary men. The next part hasn't come to me."

"Wait a minute, does the friend give him credit or not?"

"Well, I don't know, let me think on it." He kicked some rocks around and watched for signs on the horizon. A lizard came and went.

"All right, the truck is slowing down, but it's taking a while, because the driver puts it in neutral and doesn't use the brakes. In the slowing, they start talking about all they've done for each other: loans of fishing rods, building sheds on Sundays, making runs to the feed store when one of them was sick. Their conversation takes the tone of a deathbed scene. The truck finally stops and conversation ends. They get out and walk in separate directions. One starts to get some tears, but the other just stares at the ground, thinking there's nothing for him out here, but he begins to wonder what makes him so certain."

Charlie became still, like a standing stone in Scotland.

"It's just imaginary men you know. You can make anything happen."

"All right, you've got me going. I'm going to say the friend gives credit, they get back in the truck and drive off, and that starts a conversation about looking down a straight road until it narrows to a point and is gone. Some day, I swear, I'm going to make a version where men and roads and trucks aren't even part of the story."

We discussed the matter until the sun began to burn. I was heartened when Charlie announced our stories had overlapping parts. He said I was dead right about the tense, uncertain aim of the soothing hand. He was less certain about the men never taking their eyes off the road. He thinks their eyes go everywhere, but that was one of the things they weren't ready to know. I was wrong about the pickup truck coming next. What came was just a little wind kicking up a dust devil. Charlie smiled like a mentor does, telling me he was messing with me a little, and not to worry about being right, since whatever came to mind was worthy of attention.

"I used to worry about who will pick me up, get a little hopeful, but most people pass me like I'm a rock and nothing else. I learned not to worry. It's too confusing."

Since questions were in the air, I asked him why he came out here to do his thinking. I shivered in the asking while he dug his hand into his jacket for something that used to be there. The motion itself was like a ballad, a story hidden in his way of bringing out his empty hand. He used the hand to support his neck and leaned his head as far back as it would go. I thought this was probably the way his mother held him on the first day of his life—to have a good look at him and welcome him to the world. I figured he needed to let his head be cradled in his own hand, to see if this might bring his mother back. It was my turn to look down, to respect his privacy. He must have sensed my need to look away, but only looked harder into me.

"Where I end up for the night depends on if I have to move on. I don't do so well around people if they talk to me all at once. That's what I like about you. You don't rush me."

He stared over my right shoulder, twenty degrees above the horizon. "My wife knows when I'm restless, and goes to do some prayer. She puts me to bed just right, better than I can do for myself."

He must have read my next question from my eyes and said her name was Celina. He said it so softly, we saw into her worries like they were hovering above the horizon. I saw where he was looking, saw a shimmering there, and he said, "I know," to the shimmering; it made him sad, and I was sad too.

Charlie played with time and fate. He told me his goal was to stay alive until he saw evidence for a life when everybody stopped trying so hard to wreck things. He wanted a world where the important things weren't taken from a man. He's known too many people who didn't say they were dying, but didn't rise from the sagebrush to announce that living was a larger cause.

His food was gone. I pulled a bag of chips from my backpack, but he asked, "Got a cigarette?" I told him no, because I tried smoking but I was a swimmer and it wasn't worth the loss of breath and coughing all the time. He smiled.

"It's all right, I go to a place for water too," but he couldn't elaborate because fate was coming in the form of a semi-trailer truck.

Charlie tried to wave the trucker down using both hands in a friendly gesture. The trucker didn't stop, but the wind from the truck lifted the bag of chips right out of my hand, thirty feet up, tracing a perfect arc in the New Mexico morning. The bag drifted down, while we held, for its entire flight, our judgments and sins in abeyance. We came to the moment together. It was the moment between the strike of a match and the lighting of a chapel candle. Our remembrance of last night brought us down to the pavement edge. He lifted his head to speak before I thought to lift mine.

"I've been waiting for a sign, and now I see two: that truck didn't swerve to hit me, and I didn't jump in front of it like I planned on yesterday."

I was a kid, not an angel or a sage. I told him I was glad on both accounts. I declared him wise, told him I didn't want him to die, that the men in the imaginary pickup truck were on the verge of seeing something incredible, beyond fear, and they'd need him in the desert silence. I told him he had a gift and a sorrow beyond the figuring, and said:

"You can't just leave those guys in the middle of a story. I won't either." I added two more observations, respecting Charlie as the master of signs.

"That trucker wasn't the one you need. Plus, I saw your love when you said the word, Celina." I added, "You know, maybe that bag still has some chips in it."

Charlie walked over to the bag like an attorney examining Exhibit A, and found my speculation true. We shared what remained in the bag, witnessed by the morning. He spoke to the road itself, the sagebrush, and finally to me, announcing it was time he set out for home.

He didn't use the road, but took sure straight steps across the open land in the direction of Socorro. I yelled to the back of him,

"I'm naming a star after you. I'm calling it Nightcloud. It's short for Charles Charlie Nightcloud. You've got more to do here than you know."

I knew he heard me since he raised a stiff right hand while walking away. He held it up there for twenty steps or more, then raised the other hand, laced his fingers to support his tired neck, and kept on walking. He walked that way until I couldn't see him anymore. He didn't turn and he didn't pause, just like a man with special purpose.

A Summoning of Gifts to Wet Ankles

It takes determination to find the beach at Camel's Point. The portal from Pacific Coast Highway hides in dense shrubs, but a twisting feast of narrow stairs is there, a descent in a thicket fair. I've come a hundred times, a thousand more in dreams. Mornings hold you in the arms of sandstone bluffs. The smallest mood is amplified while the outer world is silenced, so every visit offers a double shot of you. Not everyone likes it here. A singular thought will not endure, and glances off unsure fragments of your past. There ought to be a sign on the highway: *Spirits Speaking from Rocks may be Unsettling.* With any ocean swell at all it's a mean shore-break, not a friendly water entry. Angular backwashes can sweep you to the mouth of a wave. I discuss the matter with elegant terns and indifferent gulls. Sand crabs offer a chorus of yes, as an exposed army between waves. Sandpipers are never fooled, and take their fill in the dimpled sand. I'm the lifeguard, eight feet up in an open plywood tower that's white-washed once a year. When the marine layer of fog is in, a wind language speaks in a restless drone, vibrating the underside of physical things. The outline of a camel rests on the north end, though I insist it's a sphinx. I consult it, lean toward it, as it watches over tide pools. The shoreline is a fresh canvas each morning. I haven't spoken to anyone in four hours.

Nobody trained us for quiet times. I invent a game: imagine every small question is profound. Ask me the ocean temperature and I'll answer, but I make it a Zen riddle. Ask about tides and I'll speak of the witnessing moon. I invent a language of hums to mirror the ocean moods.

The terrible 3:00 glare brings a headache, as my eyes are owned by the sea. It's fended off by the 5:00 glow, when people become majestic statues. Freeze this: I rescue a child being thrashed in a wave just right for humbling. His mother watches in horror. I bring him to her. She lifts him and lets him melt into her. Both are crying.

The mother sees the small distance between a breath held and a child lost. Her natural ways make a child of me. I make up private prophesies: *this lad will feel a soothing presence even in barren places.* Pelicans argue this point, passing parallel to shore. *Come fly with us instead,* say the brown pelicans. There's a shipwreck down the beach: a couple having a fight. All the room in the world, but they scream at each other nose-to-nose in a special category of drowning. Dogs bark at something moving in a pile of seaweed: a living thing in a tangled clutch. Gulls gather and peck the helpless creature. Nothing from the sea is wasted. *Come fly with us instead,* say the brown pelicans.

I dive through a wave to reach a swimmer panicking in a nasty turbulence. He's out of fight, but manages this: *Don't worry about me, Jesus has me.* I'm afraid I can't debate his point, so I pull him in. Now I've done it, destroyed the fabric of knowable life. I'm no trace of a hero to a man embarrassed to let another man give him a hand. Did I save the Anti-Christ? Did Jesus send him for me, or me for him, or is life just the way it is?

Bewilderment is second cousin to action, but explains why ocean lifeguards seek the certain salty perfection of sunflower seeds by the thousands, when the ocean is drenched in eternal salt. Salt: softening, tingling, inward-seeking, always speaks through skin.

A ten year old boy has a minor jellyfish encounter. He's brought to me as if to high court by a not-so-gentle mother. She rants as if I allowed the terrible event. His pain disappears, but the mother amps up, which of course makes the boy cry. She reminds me I'm not a doctor, and drags the tender child from his unfinished sand-castle, wrenching his arm up the stairs like she hates him along with the rest of the universe. He won't keep his castle in his memory as a magnificent gift to the tide. Here I come with another prophesy: *he won't tell his mother about his next injury, since she will have little thought of comforting him anyway. He'll wonder, maybe ten years into a numb marriage, what the hell he did wrong.*

I'm back in my tower staring at his unfinished castle. I have no filing cabinet for this. I long for the day last June, when an eerie fog settled in so thick the gulls called to each other in shrill troubled voices. The world turned brilliant white. Sea lions were crying and the day belonged to lamentations.

I'm in love with the Japanese woman who comes on the quiet days. We never speak; we have this great respect. She crouches at water's edge, telling her life to the shells and sea glass, summoning these gifts to wet ankles in long shadows. The wind language tells me the woman comes here to be with her mother, who died when she was born. I ask the evening sun to cast her mother's face on the sandstone bluffs in a perfect breadth of grace. It answers in oranges and reds: *something needs forgiving; she must give herself permission to claim her birth.* She finds a shell she fancies, sends a kindred nod to me, then leaves the shell to the cleansing brine and takes the narrow stairs. I've loved her in a hundred lives, a thousand more in dreams. Here's the other thing about Camel's Point; lovers come when my day is done, waiting for night under indigo blankets, when every grain of sand becomes a shimmering star.

Precipice

Percy Malone just left this world. Felipe Aldana called with the news, with a hitch in his voice and a little hope too, that the remaining members of the Willard Jr. High School Band would still remember Percy.

Percy, of course, Percy. Who could forget him? Our lone tuba player fifty years ago, with his oversized glasses and fidgeting ways, at home in a shirt one size too large. No one ever called him Percival, but the name might have fit, due to the noble way he held himself when he was the shortest in our crowd. After adolescence he shot up to six-foot-three, but I knew him from before.

While Felipe broke the news, my fingers pressed the phone the way I used to work the valves on my beat-up trumpet. *Where's my trumpet now?* I asked myself, with a sudden need to hold the cool brass beauty. After the call, it felt like Percy came with me on the search. We looked under the bed, behind boxes in the garage, and found it in the hall closet under a cotton blanket. Just thinking about him made us come together again, two kids banging through the house on a mission, the same way we used to look for our hidden stash of bottle rockets.

I raised my trumpet and aimed the bell toward a window of glass and time. My first offering was a raspy G note. It was sad, but so was I. Riding on its ragged edge was an addendum to the chronicles of Willard Jr. High, a breath away from telling. I knew I could do better, so I warmed the mouthpiece in my hand and raised the bid to a C, and made it be for Percy, and the whole Willard band.

The mouthpiece wanted more, so I held the note as long as I could, until the twelve-year-old version of me was transported to a windy Tuesday in May, when Mr. Sanders drew the lot to be our substitute conductor for the day. It was 1963, and a Santa Ana wind was brewing, picking up speed, banging through the canyons, racing time itself and winning. Inside the brick and stucco building, we couldn't hear the howls outside. I was second trumpet behind the saxophones. The trombones held court to my left, and Percy, who was exactly one-third the size of his instrument, sat behind me, next to the kettledrums.

The girls were a foot taller than the boys, but it felt like a two-foot difference. We were leaving childhood, on a precipice, in a suburban neighborhood insulated by post-war hope, surrounded by tens of thousands of fertile acres that made Orange County rich in grapefruit, oranges, lemons, watermelons and strawberries. Country roads were unlighted, cutting through untouched hills of manzanita and cactus on their way to un-crowded beaches. I will go there now.

None of us looked beyond the coming hour, and nothing diluted the opening speech from Mr. Sanders. His soft tenor voice still rings from the podium of the music building. Here he comes, sailing the currents of time.

"I teach math. I have no idea how to read music, much less to conduct a band. I hope the ability to conduct will come to me in a crescendo of intuition, like a welcome flood. Did you ever wish for something but needed others to make it come to pass? I'm lousy at babysitting. Please don't reduce me to that."

We were a band of thirty, captive in a rare moment, an adult talking to us like we were sailors on the same ship. Incredible, his talk of a crescendo, confident we'd understand.

"Let's cross the threshold between wish and reality. For this hour, I'd like to forget math and become what I'm doing. All of you know your instruments. I won't have time to ask your names."

Mr. Sanders was an awkward man, so we gave him credibility. He was forty or so, lean, with short brown hair and a whisper of stubble, wearing the obligatory short-sleeved plaid shirt of the era. We weren't prepared for an adult to introduce himself with a confession or a plea, but there it was, a moment that stretched our boundaries. We took our instruments from damaged cases and tuned-up with grace notes of curiosity.

Musical ancestors came to us. *Lento*—they breathed us in as we settled into our chairs. *Fortissimo*—the old ones rushed us the moment we opened a page. This must be why we never felt alone in the music room. We never stopped to wonder how Margarita came to inhabit the flute, or why Brian took to the xylophone like it was part of his skin.

Our mood was in a minor key the day that Sanders came. The show-offs didn't show off, and deferred their craft to the serious among us, especially Hikani, second piccolo, who wore a yellow ribbon in her hair. I loved her assembly of position, her delicate turn of the page, a quarter-note shy of adolescence, perfect between seven and seventeen, waiting for an emotion she could call her own. I was keen to hear her speak my name, which happened in four more years, but in the moment, I worried about her sitting in front of a man who couldn't hide his angst. He faced us as if we were jurors and he was on trial for crimes of omission.

Hikani was flooded with anxiety while Sanders studied the music. She couldn't tell his anxiety from hers. Everything was conflated; his confusion felt the same as shame. It was like he'd been left alone with the Rosetta Stone, thinking himself pathetic for not decoding the symbols on the spot. Hikani wanted to disappear, but I wanted to comfort her with a touch that was not to be, for she was thirteen, way out of my league, since I was only twelve.

I also wondered if anyone ever helped Sanders learn anything as a child. He seemed to reside in such self-criticality that every curiosity was required to pass through a glaring sense of inadequacy. I wondered if math was safe for him because there was a sequence leading to answers he could defend.

He raised the baton for several seconds, looking up at his hands as if they weren't connected to the rest of him. We saw from his expression he was looking beyond time, through the cinder block walls, beyond the sycamore trees and the green track field, past the city limits and all the algebraic solutions he held as proof there is such a thing as a right answer. All these images drifted in our collective, mixing, carving a question in our minds. Should the Willard Jr. High School Band let him in? We left it to our leaders, the fourteen-year-olds. The rest of us were too confused. Mr. Sanders might have been the USA itself, becoming self-aware in the early sixties, troubled without knowing the trouble, fearful, watching something breaking down while trying to act normal.

Sanders didn't want us to see he was sad, but some of us saw that it was so, reflected in his distorted image in the great brass tuba. He patted his shirt pocket as if to place the feeling there, and then put the baton down as gently as one might handle a newborn. His emotions were in our care. At Willard, we tried to give people an honest rendering. In a fumbling minute, he spoke again, and I swear he became an adagio.

"Life throws people together in strange ways, doesn't it? This moment serves as a fine example. Would one of you start this music, please? Someone please show me how to conduct. I cannot read music. I don't know about rhythm. I am lost."

None of us knew how to respond. We didn't know that adults could be suddenly terrified and all their efforts to cover it up would fail. We thought we were the experts in such matters. Trouble was, Mr. Sanders couldn't imagine himself conducting, and wasn't a man who could pretend. I had the precocious thought that nobody encouraged him to pretend and that was part of his sadness. I imagined him finding a pirate costume when he cleaned out his room for college, still unopened in his bottom drawer.

When nobody spoke, Mr. Sanders started to sweat. A few of us thought he was ill, and started to raise a tentative hand, but no hand rose until Julia Fillmore, our only female trombone player, reassured him that everything was OK. She told him it takes years to learn anything worthwhile. This made him smile, nervously, only to freeze up again.

In junior high school, before they called it intermediate or middle school, we entertained a narrow assumption that one teacher was merely a version of other teachers: big people with a certain scent and manner. It was implicit that adults were not allowed to have ever been like us in any way. Likewise, we couldn't imagine becoming like them. Of course, teachers were forbidden to presume a life outside the classroom.

The exception was our librarian, Mrs. Lambert, who had a rubber arm, and was therefore the subject of endless speculation. Like how did she put on her skirt or change the sheets? We exchanged ideas on how this came to pass, and shared our theories about what we'd do with a rubber arm of our own. Some of us would have preferred an arm made of wood, a steel claw, or a giant butterfly net. Of course, there were a few cruel persons in the school. Jimmy Fagan went around bragging that he stuck a pin in her arm when she wasn't looking, but nobody believed him since he made up shit all the time. He criticized everybody but himself, saying we were stupid for being in band. He would have loved to pound the crap out of me just for being alive. I developed an invisibility cloak when he was anywhere near.

More to the core of humanity, most of us declared Mrs. Lambert showed courage in being a regular person who happened to have a rubber arm. So when Mateo Camacho, our drummer, blew his right hand off with a huge M-80 firecracker, it was easy to take his injury as ours. This was our decency. The world could be cruel, but we weren't much in it yet. We were busy in the music room, and Mateo found a way to keep on drumming, inventing his own style.

The prospect of losing a limb or a life in Vietnam was only five years away, far from our radar screens. We'd seen photos of a lynching, and of Ruby Bridges in 1960, when she was only six, wearing a white bow in her hair, being escorted to a white school by U.S. Marshals in Louisiana. The hatred in the air was inexplicable to us, like news from another planet. We had our music and each other, bicycles and tennis shoes. The Space Race was making big headlines, also the Cold War. In a few years, we'd be assigned to read *Lord of the Flies* by William Golding, also *Black Like Me*, by John Howard Griffin. We looked into each other without knowing what we were seeing, but Mr. Sanders took our confusion for granted. That's when we trusted him best.

It was hard to find cynicism in the white middle class burbs, but fear was on the rise, chewing on the edges of us. Our parents weren't angry or desperate, although some were more than a tad paranoid during the cold war. Primitive forces found us all the same. If my buddies and I made a fort in our front yard, it was a territorial statement. Other kids played the intruder or called us into a contest over who could splatter soft guavas and apricots in the other's territory. It was fun at first. Then came water balloons, and ripping down each other's forts. It was a shock when the first fist flew. You see the drift, something elemental in all of us.

We didn't ride our bikes on streets where you'd get the long stares. Mexican gangs were on the rise in Santa Ana, and in all the neighboring cities. Biker gangs in Huntington Beach and Riverside had their private wars, no paradise in store. Another world existed just west of the Santa Ana River, places where the cops didn't want to go. Maybe some kind of record for murders and rapes not investigated. Up the freeway in East Los Angeles, less than an hour's drive, a fuse was lit on a bomb of black rage. But we were in the music room, practicing.

Another twist; our parents weren't especially eager for us to become adults, and rarely shared the things they said between themselves. We'd hear whispers in the bedroom. "There's something ghastly going on in the Wilson home." We'd ask, but were told it was private. Most of us accepted the dividing line. A few broke it down, with journalistic need to know.

In climbing the notes of an invisible chromatic scale, Mr. Sanders became our champion.

"If you can play sounds better than chalkboard sounds, I'll be the happiest man on earth. I tried playing drums, but I didn't have a teacher, a band, or the fire inside. I wanted to work on rockets that could go into orbit, but I remember crumpling up job applications with this very hand (right hand held high), thinking *who am I kidding, dreaming like this?* I guess I was waiting for a sign that never came. Find your own signs, or make them up from your own desires. That's my best advice on how to live a life."

I swear, the man nearly cried, but he covered it with a cough.

Three band members chuckled at the image of him crushing paper, but most of us perceived the gravity. Without need for conversation, we lifted Sanders to our private Willard praise.

At home, we watched the TV news, and read the horrors on the front page: the incremental escalation in Vietnam, the shocking justifications and atrocities. Napalm was on the way, screaming through faraway jungles. Our parents lived through WWII and Korea and wanted nothing more of war. But the winds outside were howling. The Civil Rights Movement was in full swing, while deplorable working conditions of migrant workers still existed in the fields under the Bracero program in California. North Vietnamese children, exactly our age, were learning to shoot rifles and toss grenades. Drugs were coming on strong. Our music pissed off our parents. Authority was questioned. If Formica breakfast booths could speak, they'd tell of a reckoning to come.

At Willard, we were slow to know, still fresh from duck-and-cover drills from a few years earlier—as if a wooden desk could shield us from the apocalypse of an atomic blast. In surreal calmness, teachers would read from a brochure. "Go to your knees under the desk, put your hands over your heads and clasp them tight. Whatever you do, don't look at the flash." I used to look over at my friend, Jerry. We had a language of frowns and questions under there, and mad grins too. We refused to close our eyes. We're still friends. He looks for sane solutions to energy and transportation, has deep thoughts on every subject, just like he did then.

Call us naïve, but we were cunning in our ways, reactive with a thousand moods, suspicious of being told our generation would change the world, but nobody said how. We still hear our band playing while taking morning showers.

"Can we start with a scale?" asked Sanders. We protested, weary of his avoidance, found safety in numbers, and made a collective frown.

Paula, first clarinet, took command. She turned to the bunch of us to say, "Let's show him how easy it is to conduct. I'll give the beat, Mr. Sanders. Just do the same as me."

Paula lifted her clarinet up-and-down as our proxy conductor. The piece was Sentimental Journey, bouncy and easy. For Mr. Sanders, her solution allowed the sun to shine. When he followed her lead, raising his head, he might as well have seen the ceiling of the Sistine Chapel. He used the baton at the level of his waist, as if to apologize for trying to conduct, but it was bold beyond measure. Halfway through the piece, Paula stopped her exaggerated motion, and gave him half a wink. He smiled an existential high note, relishing the moment when he had us in his grasp, and then finally lifted the baton to the level of his eyes. We were healing something terribly forlorn in him. I remember he seemed to be staring especially hard at Percy, as if to say, "See I can do this."

We'd done some good that day, playing pieces from George Gershwin, Henry Mancini, and John Philip Sousa, our best work. There came a moment when Sanders put the baton down so he could feel the music come to his open hands, wildly sweeping us into memory. When the bell rang, he said, "I'll never forget this day." We clapped for him, Percy too, dizzy with another first at Willard, secure in the chronicles now.

A few weeks later we heard another substitute was coming for the day. His name was Mr. Watson. If we said his name quickly, with emphasis on the first syllable, the sound of his name was menacing. Eunice Floyd, bassoonist, let fly a rumor he was known to be strict and unfriendly, and hated children of all ages, especially those in the seventh grade. In a small diversion from the moment of meeting him, it must be admitted his only known fault was not being the substitute teacher we loved. Our response was to scatter, like quails in the presence of a hawk. We knew how to hide our faces behind music stands. Just as quickly, we could assemble again, like a swarm of bees or a pack of wolves.

A few years later, I learned whole cultures do this too. Our band splintered in defiant anticipation of Watson, the way siblings fight bitterly over a perception of no parental love, whether it's true or not. On the surface, the fight is just about a piece of cake.

At Willard, we were famous for regrouping. Some of us, including myself, were thinking *what the hell, how will this man know what instruments we normally play, or who we even are?*

Our musings were never complete thoughts, more a collection of somatic reactions. If our regular conductor, Roland R. Schmitt, was late for practice, there was no telling what sounds and rhythms would stir us to primitive expression. We had it in us to be anarchists before we knew the word. Once, warming up during a dust storm, demonic sounds were summoned by the trombones. I remember the reply of Bruce Feinberg, playing a solo Bach andante on his flute, offering evidence of beauty and order in the midst of chaos. He had private lessons, and was one of the few of us who knew about classical music.

It wasn't until college that I learned of musical souls playing violin or piano in the Polish ghettos, knowing they were going to be killed by Nazis. At Willard, we were vessels waiting to be filled by history: horrified one moment, seduced the next, with undetermined goals.

I remember my trumpet response to the trombones—a garish off-key version of "The Star-Spangled Banner." The drummers joined the trombones and tried to drown me out. They could not, since the other trumpets joined me and the alto saxophones fell in. We had a right to speak this way, and nobody died from trying.

The 50's were gone like cotton candy while the 60's came screaming down the hall, headed straight for us.

Serious revolution was not yet in our minds. It was hiding around the corner while the frightening Mr. Watson stood there, deadpan. We couldn't find the truth of him. We were left to doubt his nature and agenda, like when a new leader shows up and announces he exists for all, but promises facile solutions with a wicked smile. Most of us didn't know about Fidel Castro until the Cuban Missile Crisis. Who were the Soviets anyway?

Before Watson approached the podium, he turned his back to look for sheets of music. Was it courage that invited half of us to change instruments? What were we defying? What was our country defending? Watson's presence signaled that freedom of speech was suspended. The same was happening in our neighborhoods. The John Birch Society was reviving McCarthyism in Orange County; our mission was to fight the spread of Communism at all costs. It was dangerous to speak otherwise. Careers and lives were destroyed by paranoia. Suddenly, patriotism meant fearing our government, along with our neighbors.

We wanted Mr. Sanders back, having no category for Mr. Watson. A psychotic belief was growing in the culture—that all threats were external, certainly not those within ourselves. So we sat, disguised, half-baked for consequences, with no one in the music room to advise us. Let it be told; the Willard Band was seeking direction, but found it in our guts.

If Watson sensed something was up, he gave no hint. Of course he must have sensed a ruse; switching seats is hardly a new trick on substitutes. Plus, it's well known that children cannot hide these things for long. Watson lifted his hands to the sky, then paused right there on purpose. He paused so long we froze in our hard pine chairs. Some of us entertained a vision of the apocalypse.

This portly man in a loose black tie made the universe boil down to him vs. us, in a flat-out standoff, a poker bluff, a gamble, with nothing clearly to win on our side.

Twenty seconds went by, with Watson posed like a vulture with nine foot wings, ready to descend on the carrion of us. He riveted us to a Dante's *Inferno* scene; his glee felt relentless, but we couldn't be sure since his tense lips wouldn't reveal the meaning of his cringe. When his arms finally came down in hopes of conducting *American Patrol*, our most loathsome piece, those of us who changed instruments sounded more horribly wrong than we could have imagined.

How can a valve trombone player make sense of a reed instrument for the first time? Some students—the ones who didn't change instruments—played along normally, although there was a mutual sense of grief. The sum of our sound was that of a forlorn animal being herded into a pen for slaughter.

This looming quality, I would soon learn, was kin to our coming war, when we would have to decide if we were for or against what was happening in Vietnam, and offer our lives when we knew so little about why.

Jeremy Storm, master of the baritone, seemed to understand sacrifice. He relished the principle in a biblical way while attempting to make the foreign flute come alive. But he formed his lips so terribly wrong around the oval opening that it appeared he would eat the instrument. How can you kiss Godzilla one moment and a hummingbird the next? His real love was the baritone. Amazingly, he pulled off an impression of normality in a valiant second effort.

All eyes focused on the lad, and the lot of us felt he won the moment. Surely, his was the most daunting challenge. It was easy to pretend you could play the cymbals or strum the upright base. But resting on Jeremy's production of an actual note on the flute, a wrong note, but close enough to the right note, was our deferral of the storm, our purchase of an extra moment of youth.

It was inevitable that Jeremy's skill did not extend to the rest of us, for the clever and devious Mr. Watson was simply waiting us out.

Miles Preston gave a laudatory effort holding the tenor saxophone correctly, as if he could play it simply because he held it right, but the result was the howl of a banshee, a screech so offensive it could not be allowed in this world. I heard he never wanted to be a dentist. His parents had that career in mind for him from the age of ten, and that's what he did for ten years after college, hating it the whole time.

I learned from another Willard friend that Miles was suicidal for quite a while, even made a few attempts. Then, with the help of kindred souls, he found support, quit dentistry, and started a senior center, where he formed a band. Somewhere along the way, he came out as gay. Go Miles! He represented a declaration that our sounds will always be our property.

Naturally, we were plenty pissed a handful of years later, coming out of the cultural bubble. Our parents grew sad, wondering if their sacrifices were even valued by their children. War was coming again. I saw their worrisome ways. Their generation worked it out in the jitterbug and swing. Soldiers came back as heroes. Our generation was trying on cool for size, staying uncoupled on the dance floor, dressing in tie-dye, letting hair grow long, taking drugs that opened or mellowed. We didn't realize we were inheriting the trauma of war within our father's silences and the ways our mothers quietly folded clothes. They worked during the war in factories. Never complained, as far as I ever heard. So strong, we didn't even know. Our parents wanted to make war as distant as possible from the families they created. Best to be humble, I told myself, when I was a little older.

But I was not humble that day in May, during the great stare-down of 1963. I abandoned the trumpet and chose my muse to be the tuba. From the back of the room, I watched the spotlight descend on Flordeliza Gomez. Bless her. She proved too shy to pull a trick on a strange adult. By staying with her clarinet, she gave the guilty among us a faint bit of cover. Flor was a rare person who played consistently, no matter who was at the podium. The rest of us had little interest in maturity. If we didn't like a substitute, we'd go limp, or play a little bit flat. But she was solid, true to her music no matter what. I heard she became an administrative law judge. The world needs more people like Flor.

Although she was on our side, Flor suffered a moment of failed containment; a fateful giggle rose from her, in short bursts, to a point where she might explode. It was then that Watson knew for sure we were having him on.

He grunted like a wounded bear and fixed his stubby hands, his monstrous hands, on his hips. Catalina Martinez, one of the brave switchers in the front row, turned sideways to Watson, and told me later she was thinking of places in Florida where the ground just opens up and whole houses go in. To be taken in by a sinkhole was a fate she fully expected, but since it didn't come to pass, she started privately saying her Rosary in the trembling reaches of her mind. Nobody knew she lived in deeper fears, was being molested at home, for she never told a soul.

Tell me if you know fear this way? It wasn't just Catalina. Some band members had very mean fathers. Not just a little mean, but so violent and unpredictable their children flinched if a teacher so much as raised a hand to adjust their glasses.

Those students had a way of walking, hugging the certainty of walls between classes, and were vigilant all the time. That was the power of Watson's glare; it made puddles of Michael P. and Cyrus

S., both trumpeters to my left. In contrast to their fathers, Watson didn't actually hit them, but they reacted as if he had. Of course they never switched instruments. Why take such a risk? I never heard about my fellow trumpeters in later life. I hope they became fathers with the patience to build strong things slowly, to counteract how fast a person can crumble.

It dawned on me, squirming in my chair; I was the ringleader. I was the first to switch instruments. Watson figured out who was guilty by analyzing our faces, taking his maddening time about it, observing our pathetic failures of sustained eye contact.

Some of us had medium strict parents, and learned the strategy of looking downward in feigned apology. This worked surprisingly well for a few, and I resolved to carry no judgments for fellow musicians. A few gave up the ruse and changed back to their original instruments before Watson could single them out.

He seemed to let them escape. Down the road of time, I was told a version of this worked for some people in China under Chairman Mao: a simple matter of renouncing independent thought and memorizing the Chairman's exact words or suffer horrible humiliation, not to mention prison or death. Just conform and you might be spared. At Willard, we also learned about Genghis Kahn, Julius Caesar and Napoleon Bonaparte; well, at least we learned enough to be curious later. It was thought to be helpful to our formative minds to show us black-and-white enactments on the TV series, *You Are There*. It takes a special teacher to make history relevant to the twelve-year-old mind, and we had one in Mr. White. I think it was deliberate that he sat at his desk pretending to grade papers while playing an episode called "Hitler Invades Poland." Actual footage was used in that episode. He wanted us to see it without being coached. Nobody filled that silence. The bell rang, but suddenly it had no meaning.

We were also learning about Einstein and relativity, so I wondered, even before becoming a teenager, why can't the future visit from time to time? Especially if time itself can bend. Nobody could give me a good explanation, so I made it so. I decided the future could visit me as it pleased. There was no such TV series called *You Are Going to Be Here Someday. Good Luck!* That would have been my title I suppose.

Oh, and in Cambodia, a handful of years after our Willard days, there would be no principle of relativity, or mercy from the Khmer Rouge. You were either a mindless worker or you were declared a threat, and had to be willing to turn in your family members and best friends. Even then you would likely be shot in the head, or if you survived, you had to live with something arguably worse than death. Having a profession, an education, could get you killed. What was waiting for us outside the music room? The future stirred the notes on our music pages.

When Watson's eyes found me, I was living in the convoluted vastness of a tuba, where a young man can find a bit of solace. The instrument is so big that if someone tries to hit you, they'll likely dent the instrument and hurt their hand, but miss your person.

Here's a retrospective confession; we didn't give Watson much of a chance. He didn't give us one either, leading things off with his menacing glare. We fell to a frozen state, just as some students did when a substitute parent was suddenly on the scene.

One band member, trombonist H. Bartholomew, described his stepdad simply as a man who sat in a favorite chair and read his preferred newspaper. That's all H would say on the topic of his stepfather. H was known for his brevity. I asked him to tell me more about the chair his stepdad used, not the man, and he liked my question so much we became friends, but we never exchanged ideas in more than five carefully chosen words at a time, like there was a rule, but we never really crafted a rule, and had no idea why it seemed important. He was my most enigmatic friend in band. Sticking to the *rule of five*, once I said, "The clarinets were sharp today," and he said, "All mimsy were the borogoves," quoting Lewis Carroll. When you play by *the rule of five*, clarifications are not allowed.

Back to the moment I've been evading. Watson summoned a huge breath and announced he was done with our silliness, but he uttered the word with a gigantic, deliberate lisp, along with a goofy twist of his upper lip, so we suddenly didn't know if he was lisping for real, or was just getting started in a display of comedic genius. We were on the verge of hating him—as much we were supposed to hate Communism.

We weren't prepared for Watson to emerge as a man capable of comedy. Just as likely, he was dangerous, keeping us off balance. My dad, a journalist, was telling me about the rise of Papa Doc Duvalier in Haiti, who had his private army make thousands of people "disappear." The man gave friendly, convincing interviews on the world stage. Plus, my dad was still smarting, along with his whole generation, from being duped by Smiling Joe Stalin, who won the support of Americans by an acting job, all the while hiding the slaughter of millions of his own people. Look what happens if you don't play along in the real world. Mr. Watson was just a warm-up.

Watson was menacing enough for us at the time, and upped the ante by transforming himself to an impulsive, foaming creature. Plus, he added a weird little gesture with his hands, as if he was talking to a consultant in his mind, but only through his hands. Like he was asking his hands if they should wring our necks and his hands were saying *yes*. Although the budding psychologist in me was curious, my attempt to figure Watson out was nullified the moment he said, "You," pointing at me with a finger as straight as a dagger, "Play a C and play it right."

I tried. I swear I tried. But my version of the C on the tuba was the sound of a moose stranded in a New York subway. I discovered how the twelve-year-old mind is exquisitely capable of creating visions of doom. I longed for a dissociated state, a fugue, and had to call upon future knowledge; a bargain exchanged in the pawn-shop of my mind for a sliver of relief.

Fast-forward to graduate school in psychology. I learned how fugue states, though rare, can actually happen: a variant of trau-matic adaptation. We read about a guy who kept turning up in psychiatric units in different states, with no idea who he was or how he ended up in the hospital. Experts checked him out and concluded he wasn't brain damaged or a sociopath. Nobody could agree as to his pathology. He had some trigger that would make his identity too much to bear, and he managed to get to other cities and find jobs, with no recall of his former life. Everyone, especially women, thought he was simply a nice man who was a little lonely. Eventually, he'd fall into unresponsive states and end up in the hos-pital. He never had a cross word for anyone.

The patient was said to be congenial. The doctors tried to prove he was lying, that he hated authority figures, had undercur-rents of rage, was brutalized as a child, but he'd say something like, "You're all very nice, but I really have to go now." He didn't present any physical danger to himself or others, so they had to let him go.

That's him; that's the guy I wanted to be the moment I couldn't play the C for Watson. It was a simple matter of not being the kid he was talking to, not being me at all. If only I had better presence of mind, I could have lied, saying we always change instruments for the first half of band practice, with a goal of appreciating each other's challenges. But our tension was too personal. It was time to take the fall for the troops. I took a piece off the tuba and put a rubber fart-imitator on the open end, the kind twelve-year-old guys carried for general purposes, and let her rip, with no damn C in mind.

For a few seconds, going down this way seemed elegant; pride mixed with utter confusion of purpose. It's a mix that's been known to yield, on summer days, the image of a beautiful flat rock skipping on the surface of a placid lake, suspended in time before the final sinking moment. The laughter among my peers made the music room rattle for a full minute. It was my finest moment at Willard.

Watson, of course, was unmoved, and handled it masterfully, waiting patiently for the last chuckle to fade. I'd come up against a professional.

You could hear a drop of spit from any brass instrument. Nobody took a breath. Watson pointed his dagger finger at me and swept it slowly across the room, pointing to my place of exile. I was banished to the soundproof practice room to ponder my crime in silence. To tell this part, I have to call on the future again, to my friend who busted some windows of a bank during the late sixties and was thrown in a grungy jail in San Francisco. They finally let him go, but he told me he was never the same after that. I don't know what to make of the visitation, except that the stakes get higher as you defy authority in the adult world.

I was stone-faced, arms at my sides, not exactly repentant, but close to regretting it, since I didn't know what was coming next and had good reason to fear being sent to Principle Scott, not to mention my dad. Back then, when I got out of line in P.E. class, there were standard consequences. You ran laps in the hot sun, and then reported to the coach's office to be hit so hard on the butt by a size fourteen tennis shoe, you'd have tears but it was vital not to show the coach he hurt you. You had to show that you took it, and that was the only way to get through the experience. The bastard would hit us in groups of three for added humiliation. I had bruises for a week, but never told my parents. I learned that one student's father gave him some old-fashioned justice, but it never took away the sting in my mind.

In the practice room (mind you, not some Moroccan jail), I wasn't counting on feeling sad, but after about fifteen minutes, there was nothing sadder than being close to my band while not being able to hear them. I invented Mahler, and my own version of Tchaikovsky's Pathetique. I looked at the dented instruments around the room, and the dents stared back at me. I remember the little holes in the soundproof walls, and wanted the lights off, but didn't want the darkness.

Before the merciful bell, the sound of music penetrated. There they were: my band, my kin, speaking to me. With one in the penalty box, the Willard Band was playing a Souza march with absolutely no heart, hitting all the notes under threat. The clarinets hissed at Watson. The trombones were flat on purpose, and the flutes were hellish shrill. When Watson called for the trumpets to soar, they crashed his mind like wild boars. He forced them all to play, but they weren't going to play as if they loved music. I smiled as big as the kettledrum, and wasn't alone anymore.

Watson didn't let me out until all the other students left, squeezing off the possibility my cohorts might signal some version of triumph. His eyes were fixed on a music page when he said he'd remember me for a long time, a very long time indeed. I've seen his hands in nightmares.

Vietnam was gearing up. Soon, we'd go electric, rogue, protesting the rising sun, challenging the ways of parents. A few died young or disappeared. Some went off to war. All of it rocked our families. So much fell apart, I don't even know. The Willard Band was never formally photographed to my knowledge. Our class picture was a black-and-white panorama, absent all the names.

Felipe Aldana, who called with the news of Percy's death, was a percussionist by some natural genetic mix. He said Percy passed quietly in the middle of the night, that he'd been ill for quite a while. Word was going around. Felipe asked if there was anyone else we might think to tell? I decided to tell the world.

Somewhere in the conversation, Felipe said that Percy had a stepdad from the age of eight. I didn't meet Percy until we were twelve. It's funny, Percy only spoke of having a dad—never mentioned a stepdad. It didn't matter; none of us paid close attention. We were busy making inventions—important things that could float or fall apart spectacularly. We made skateboards out of roller skates before they were mass-produced. The long notes of friendship were stitched into our fidgeting ways. Our jeans were full of dirt from where we fell and we didn't care one bit.

It turns out that Percy told Felipe his stepdad was a math teacher named Leopold Sanders, and Percy dreaded the prospect of ever seeing him in class, as that would be way too weird.

"How stupid is that name?" Percy once declared. It turned out Mr. Sanders was our substitute band teacher in 1963, and his opening speech was meant for Percy all along. The Santa Ana winds were just the backdrop, carrying dust on out to sea.

We never knew it, could not have known it. Felipe said the family was having a rough patch, barely speaking in the home. Sanders seized the opportunity, killed the dread of his doubt when he spoke to his stepson in front of a bunch of goofy kids. We had not yet read the classics, could not have known we were acting as a Greek Chorus. Willard comrades paved the way for Sanders to have a second start with Percy. The family gradually harmonized, according to Felipe, who chronicled such matters.

The culture splintered beyond belief. Percy didn't get drafted. He spent his life helping children whose bodies didn't work so well.

The man had values, and the most spectacular succulent garden I've ever seen. He says it's easy: just put a cutting in some nurturing earth, give it water and sun, and get out of the way. I hear his tuba now; the approximate notes were always enough. He refused to own a gun.

I'm putting my trumpet back on the shelf after hitting the C that's in my mind. Something remains in motion and it's more than just the wind; it must be the ancestors, calling us back once more. The fragrant citrus groves were paved over long ago. The shellfish are gone from the beaches. The open fields have vanished, leaving a monotony of suburban homes, evenly spaced with tidy fences. All I offer is the clarion C. Faces of invisible people drive there now, talking on cell phones, stuck in the commute. Only the ocean looks the same on the surface, minus a billion fish.

Percy Malone has left this world and May has turned to June. Time: hot beacon of an offshore lighthouse, shines round again too soon.

The Sages of West 47th Street

It was 1974, in Manhattan, when cabbies were killed for a pock-etful of cash or less. Most of the veteran drivers were depleted, refused to work the nights, and locked themselves in a vault of untold stories. Their faces were etched with trenches, like they couldn't use their face anymore to register an expression, even if they felt one coming on.

I was among the new drivers. A black leather jacket might have helped me look the part, but I didn't own one. California was stamped across my presence: longhaired blond kid, wearing tennis shoes in February. Blending was a futile thought that never made it to a full thought anyway, since the main persuasion was hunger for the night to come and take away the shadows. We gathered out-side the garage at shape-up in late afternoon, on West 47th Street, waiting for our yellow cabs to be assigned.

I had no category, no summation for what I felt in the presence of Jerome. My unsettled thoughts flowed to him unfiltered, and returned in a gentle rain. He'd offer an irony or a kindness to any-one around. The effect was to invite us fellow drivers to breathe a little slower, look up at the sky, and smile at our confusion.

Jerome had a thick brown jacket and deep brown eyes to match. I never saw the top of his head since he always wore a Greek fisherman's cap. He never told his past, so I made one up: escapee from a cult, and before that another escape from a family that expected too much. In between, maybe a bit of graduate school. Theology, I thought, or physics. He balanced curiosity with calmness and the mixture spilled easily to the world, but the quality I remember most was his ability to speak directly to the anxiety in a person.

On a shivering day, after witnessing a string of inhumanities on the streets, I told him I couldn't tell the difference between the dread stirred up by the wind or the urgency of sirens all around.

"Is it me, or is the city falling?" I asked. He seemed to know me from another realm.

"If I were you, and maybe I am, I'd remind myself of the good in my intentions. We start out thinking we're just driving a person where they want to go. But it's not that simple. Half the time we take them to a place of resignation, where they're trapped but don't know it, or flat out sad in the going. Passengers think they're unseen, but we see them if we look. We think we're faceless to them, but they can see us too if they look. I used to worry about what to say. I think the better question is what version of myself to bring. Then I'll know what to say. I hope you make fifty bucks in tips tonight. Be safe." I wished him the same and more.

A few words from Jerome could break our isolation. Our workplace was the enclosed space of a car, with dozens of people in random succession: one minute a jitterbug, the next minute Brahms. Jerome was a lingering benevolence, concrete at the same time, a chain smoker and a regular guy. We all feared being shot or robbed, but some of us feared futility. Jerome fought it by playing his boom box on low volume, ballads from the south, blues or

Bach, or dance music. He'd close his eyes and go right where he wanted. You can't teach that.

A few weeks after I came on the scene, a fellow named Richard joined us: tall sphinx with wild hair and a trademark scarf. It was debatable how much of him was there. He'd listen to our stories of the night before and fix himself to talk, but hesitation got to him and he cocked his head to somewhere far. Like me, he was a little bewildered. None of us asked how our life paths led to driving a cab. It didn't seem important. We were an assortment, marbles in a jar.

I suppose I told my story out of need for acceptance, how I ended up driving a cab within a week of arriving in the city, all because nobody stopped me. I covered up my ignorance by asking customers what route they would like to take if the trip wasn't a straight shot. It's not like anyone said, *thanks for asking, but you really ought to know that.* It worked surprisingly well.

I'd hitchhiked from California and stayed with a college friend on the Upper West Side, pausing on an eastward drift toward Europe. The city had a taste I couldn't name, a gritty, crumbling persistence, nothing like my homes in Southern California and San Francisco. Trains blew a hot gale through choking tunnels. Some of the subway clocks were broken, but folks didn't look up to notice. Except for bits of space in parks, and the grey surrounding waters, New York City was a vertical cacophony, grinding in shrill collisions, like brakes wearing out on a city bus that nobody planned to fix.

I had no preconception, was running out of money, then an idea came to me the way hands bring water to the face. I'll drive a taxi and become an anonymous seeker. It was time I read *Moby Dick* again, a time to find the *Ishmael* in me, sign up on *The Pequod*, so to speak. All my cars could be like ships, and all my rides and mates would fix themselves to turning pages. The city could be *The Whale*, appearing then submerging. I could be hidden and exposed, folding and unfolding in a surreal Kabuki Theatre.

But I found there's no such thing as anonymous, since part of myself was aware.

And thoughts are only kindling, bringing a small glow before the real fire comes. I didn't know cabbies were being killed with shocking frequency, or a vicious crime wave was strangling the city. I'd driven a cab for extra money during college in suburbs of Southern California, into the barrios and bad parts of Santa Ana, Huntington Beach, Garden Grove; places where cops didn't want to go. But New York City was electric, with constant rising pressure.

I was grateful my friend offered a mat and sleeping bag in a corner of his living room. Friends of his gypsy-like roommate came and went, including a petite pale woman, an artist, when bangs were in, and jeans were rarely washed. I had interest in her, can't say why, maybe her remoteness, then she clarified her two loves were barbiturates and art. She had a premonition she would die in the middle of a painting before the age of thirty. It was something close to a wish. She wouldn't let anyone see her work.

"Why not finish the painting first?" I asked, "then you can see if it's worth dying for, and keep on painting until one image begs for another." I was the optimist, I'm sure, but her romance was with despair and she locked herself in there.

"Don't try to save me. I'm never going to be your type, surf boy."

"Saving wasn't on my mind, but with eyes like yours, the sea isn't far behind." I had no idea why I said that to her.

"Fair enough," she said, making me briefly visible, and we made a deal of distance; the sum of our connection being a few long walks. We never kissed or spoke of darkness. When we walked,

I picked up smaller leaves from our path and placed them on a stump or bench. I don't know if she noticed. It was my way of being around her. Once, she pulled her hair back and let the winter sun come find her. It never seemed a good idea to tell her I was drawn to her quietness. I had to let her go when I couldn't find a home in the dullness of her eyes, for she started adding alcohol to barbs. I wondered if I mattered to her in some unknowable way, or if her painting told. She went back to her studio across town, and wouldn't give me her number. I went off to drive a cab.

The graffiti outside was menacing and mocking, with saturated reds, black outlines, distorted faces with screaming tongues, defiance in a nest of locusts, a savage bouquet on a subway car. It was not the graffiti of the sixties, not the birth of a new age. Still, the art of the streets felt honest, a response to the decay.

Getting a hack license was an unexpected breeze. I got a NY driver's license and went to a garage, where a grizzly bear, disguised as a man, handed me a form. One thing you learn in college is how to fill out a form. They were hard-up for drivers; there would be no interview. I took a written exam showing I had memorized locations of hospitals, train stations, airports, and had to pass their five-minute physical. Suddenly I had a sponsor, Chase Maintenance Corporation: a fleet to call my own. Nobody trained me or asked if I'd ever seen Grand Central Station, which I hadn't. I pulled out of the garage, made two inexplicable right turns, and opened my life to chance.

My brethren shared similar ironies. Even Richard offered a rare elaboration.

"I like people who stare out the window. If I'm alert, they'll sense it and say something important. It's amazing what people tell. Sometimes I think I'm not even a person to them, and they suddenly say they're going to take a trip, place a bet, change a relationship, or stop drinking. They need to say it out loud. I guess they want approval, or just a little recognition." He was the most careful driver of us all, fresh from Kansas City. It was easier to be gay in Manhattan.

Then there was Rico, who never said where he was originally from, except Jamaica was one of his stops. He drove like a maniac but he was the most skillful maniac I ever saw. Behind the wheel, he looked flat out mean, but he wasn't mean around us. He had a goal of speed, making it his personal challenge to get people to their destination in the shortest time possible.

"If you don't fill a space with where you're going, somebody else will." It was Rico's philosophy. He told of an altercation. "A guy hailed me and I got there first. Yeah, I cut across a few lanes. It's what we do. Shit man, I almost got killed for it. This guy got out of his cab and broke my window. What's wrong with this town?"

None of us wanted to remind him it's the one thing you don't do to a fellow driver, cut in front when you can see he's zeroing in on a fare. There's a backlog of rage waiting to be triggered. Some of it lives in cabbies. Nobody's immune.

Richard surprised us, summoning an oblique response.

"If you drive too fast, your rider isn't going to tell."

"Tell what?" asked Rico.

"Tell their world. I collect worlds. They're always checking you out in the mirror, wondering if you're the guy to tell. They're surprised at what they say, and I'm surprised at what I say back. That's why I'm not in a hurry."

Rico debated the matter.

"Fucking no money in that, but I get your point. I guess we're different. I want them to admire my skill."

"I want to see if I'm the one," said Richard. There was always a haiku brewing in him.

I, myself, never flipped off anybody driving a taxi, too afraid of the occasional madman, remembering newspaper stories about regular people getting murdered for far less on L.A. freeways, sometimes for driving too slow. Jerome didn't flip people off either, but his belief didn't come from fear. He had elevated awareness.

"In another life, you could be the guy smashing up windows, and no matter what damage you cause, you're going to be alone in that anger." He believed consciousness is recycled. You could say he took the long view. Nobody made us pause like Jerome.

But Marcos, fresh from Argentina, came close. He was just learning English, and all of us helped him along. "I don't like scare people," he added, pointing to his own chest. He could have meant it either way, or both ways, since everything Marcos said was like a mirror.

"Jesus tells me when I'm upset. I don't know it myself. Jesus helps me." At first I fancied him in the wrong profession, and thought he'd be great teaching children to nurture a garden. A person that humble can be chewed up by this job. Maybe not, maybe he was the best of us and could transform common rage into compassion. He made us want to protect him, the way he kept touching his chest, as if to anchor his heart to a tentative hope that others had a heart too. "I like drive," he said, putting his hands in the air at ten o'clock and two.

Jerome reassured him, "Good man." It was the perfect thing to say to Marcos, again and again. All of us nodded in agreement.

Emmanuel, from Nigeria, declared that driving a taxi was the best job on earth. He had a new baby, proved it with pictures, and said his wife was proud of him. His health was excellent, his humor broad, his affection genuine, without a hint of cynicism. The rest of us had a bit of envy. He wondered why people complain about anything, like his customer who vented for twenty blocks about being passed over for promotion. Emmanuel shook his head, saying the guy gave a lousy tip.

"Your punishment for not agreeing with him," concluded Jerome. Emmanuel didn't understand the concept and continued.

"He had no idea how he sounded to me. I came from dirt floors, but my mother loved me. I'll bet he came from a rich family, but nobody wanted him. That's why he's poor inside." Jerome took the matter under consideration using two hands to make an imaginary cup.

"Emmanuel, old soul, you know you hold the world together. You've known it for a hundred incarnations. Sometimes it's a burden. You'll be fine if you don't spill the water."

But we didn't know, not exactly. Jerome had us all figured in a vast cycle of reincarnation, but he never said he was Buddhist. He borrowed from all the great traditions. He must have escaped a hundred prisons. Nothing was coincidence; we were given tasks of compassion, fated to live in each other's skin and the hardest part about being human is to hold back judgment. Besides, what is there to judge about the infinite? His boom box was as sacred as any other material thing to him: temporary, like the cars we were assigned. He said our stories were ancient.

Two weeks into the job, around midnight, a prostitute flagged me down west of Times Square, and informed me of a kindred link between her kind and mine. "How about a ride home, no meter, for a quick hand job. I just got ripped off. I'm broke. The asshole even stole my coat." I thought of my previous customer, his unexpected tip, and the life lesson only minutes before. The poor guy was in a daze, wandering a few blocks from a hospital. The air around him was grave, for his wife of thirty years had died within the hour. In the sacred moment, I was all of humanity to him.

"She's gone, she's gone, my Maggie's gone." I could see him crying in my mirror, and sat with him in the snow. I was sorry he had to do the practical thing and tell me where he wanted to go. I was thinking he needed a church or a friend. The simple became the impossible. He wasn't sure at first, then asked me to take him home, like I should have known the address. He had to reach for it in his mind and it hurt him to say the numbers.

I drove with no quickness, no sharp turns, respectful. But he didn't want to arrive.

"Don't pull over, not yet, just go around the block a few times. I'm not ready to go inside."

"Of course, I understand," but it was too much to understand, and I summoned the kind of silence I learned during long hitch-hiking rides across the Midwest, usually from a trucker wanting company, but that didn't always mean a conversation. It's hard to explain, but it's true that presence can be an unopened book on a table. While driving my man around the block, he used the trembling voice you can only show a stranger, telling me about Maggie as he stroked her bag of clothes in a heartbreaking way, like the bag was a treasured cat who knew he was there and purred. He asked me to take the bag of clothes to a charity.

At first I said I'd be honored, but reminded him he might regret that, and to wait a little while before relinquishing anything. He had no strength to argue. I had no Plexiglas barrier in the car that night, no barrier of any kind when he reached to shake my hand. After he was inside, I warmed my hands on the car heater, turning it up full blast. Sometimes the heaters worked.

So when the prostitute was center stage, I was full of other sorrows. She needed to go fifteen blocks, not a small distance in heels. Call me a sucker, but I used the meter to keep out of trouble, and paid for her short ride. "This one's on me," I said, "I don't need any payment." Strangers helped me in a jam many times before, and Maggie was my guide.

It's true, people barf or make love in the back seat of cabs, or pull a note from their purse and read it over and over, then leave it on the seat as if it belongs to someone else. People ignore you or make you vital, resolving, dissolving, opening and shutting the door in a thousand different ways. Jerome was like an attending physician and we were eager interns, so I ventured unanswerable questions.

"Hey Jerome, what do you do when a couple is screaming at each other in the back seat and the woman tells you to let her out of the cab, but you're going fifty miles an hour over the Triborough Bridge in a storm?" By then, I valued Jerome as my mentor, a kind of a preview for psychotherapy training, only better.

He said he'd give the couple another awareness, such as, "Look, you two, my mother is dying in Baltimore. I need to think about what I want to say to her tomorrow. I see you both have a lot of passion, so I'm sure you can help me out. What should I say to comfort her before she crosses over? I'm going to miss her terribly." Jerome said it's true his mother was ill, and the couple might see beyond their destruction if he suggested a taste of loss. I needed more of his wisdom, a template, and an approach.

"Jerome, I'm sorry to hear about your mother. I imagine you by her side, tender beyond words. When the time comes, I'm sure you your presence is what matters, maybe thank her for all she's given you, and touch her so she's not alone."

He got a distant smile going, then asked what I thought of his hypothetical response to my couple.

"It's amazing the way you invited the couple to see their existential trap. So what do you do when a woman in your cab is really drunk and seductive, giving you bedroom eyes in the mirror while singing *Someday My Prince Will Come?*"

"That happened to you, didn't it?"

"Last night, both scenarios. Kind of a typical night. Also, it seems every night I have at least one fare that runs down the street without paying, usually a young man, but sometimes a young couple. Always, they're laughing when they run, like it's fun to them."

"Never chase a runner. Let Karma handle it. Not worth a bullet, plus if you leave your car for even ten seconds, someone will steal it."

"I know. I chalk it up to desperate times and cowards. With the fighting couple, I tried the direct approach, asked them to take it down a notch, and continue their fight later, as I was concentrating on the storm, the one outside. It worked, sort of. At least I got them home. But I wonder if I should have said something different."

"You're the driver, it was good you decided it was time to be seen by them."

"The singing woman had a strange sadness. I was drawn to her perfume. I could have taken advantage, but it's not me. I started to compliment her beautiful singing but when I turned around, she'd passed out in the back. Good thing the doorman helped her in. One of her shoes was missing. Why do I remember that image the most?"

"Because it's central to her novel, a *Cinderella* perversion. Not so unusual. James, you don't need to question how you're handling everything. You're decent. Look for small signs. Listen for your heartbeat. If you can find a way to stop thinking so hard, you might be a psychologist someday. All that thinking can get in the way."

Richard chimed in. "Wait a minute, you mean the woman who lives on 77th near West End Avenue? She's famous among cabbies. Perfume is Heaven Sent. I've driven her home too. Everyone knows about her, always stuffs the one shoe under the driver's seat so the cops can prove she was in your car. Always drunk, but cunning. You can be sure she took your hack license number down. Don't ever touch her. She's dangerous, has rape charges pending on at least three drivers I know about. Probably more. Cabbies call her Poison.

"My God," I said, "looks like I dodged a bullet."

"You are dangerously green, my friend," said Rico, "don't go up in Harlem for a while, thrill kill of a cabbie last night. By the way, have you ever driven *Chester the Gimp*? He dresses like he's down-and-out, and you never know where he's going to show up. Could be Queens or Brooklyn. Always rushes out in the middle of the street with his big sloppy basset hound, Wilber. He's testing us. If you ask the dog's name, he'll give you a twenty-dollar tip. If you grumble about Wilber, who smells really bad, Chester will signal him to pee in your cab. Then you're done for the night. I've heard he's a millionaire who started a mutual fund and shot himself in the leg after a bad day on the stock market. That's why we call him The Gimp. I've got a dozen other characters to tell you about."

Marcos was taking all this in and had something important to say.

"I pick up man John and he came up close and ask, *are you honest person?* And I said, *I think so, I try to be,* and he sat back in the seat all quiet. When I let him out, a gun dropped out of his coat. He got it back. That was all."

Jerome thought it was a sign. "Good man, Marcos," but it wasn't such a good world.

I only saw a few women who drove cabs back then, and had my lone accident with a gal in Greenwich Village, where I didn't know the slanting streets. It was a small collision, in a no-fault glancing way. We were both from out of state, which explained our polite exchange of information. I liked her instantly, the way she said, "Shit happens," without a trace of anger, and I swear she almost winked. I offered to take her to dinner and trade stories in a no-fault glancing way. She said her girlfriend wouldn't understand, but I was glad for the tender ending.

On days off, I'd walk for hours, and saw some beautiful portraits on smaller SoHo walls. I wanted them to be the work of the petite pale artist who disappeared. I kept twisting the world that way, and saved a single leaf from being trampled, thinking of her, holding it up the to sun. Later in the day I stumbled onto Washington Square Park. All the chess players were deep in contemplation. It heartened me to watch a genius kid playing a very old man, ninety I'd say, punching the timer and waiting. They had such great respect. Nearby was the stink of trash that had been on the streets for days, piled on the curb or high against buildings. There were pockets of ongoing strikes, gearing up for something big. Services were unreliable. If a fire truck was stuck in traffic, siren blaring, nobody pulled to the side.

Late one afternoon, a man had collapsed in the middle of Broadway and 108th, with pedestrians walking right past. I was locked in traffic in the opposite direction, watching cars honking, as if they would have been fine with the closest driver running over him: a man in a grey jacket, face on the asphalt, you or I. Everyone was furious at the inconvenience. This world can be dark and you can't un-see it. Apparently he'd been hit by a car and the driver sped off. The streets were paralyzed, the city howled. Finally, a person crouched to check on him. Someone yelled to the owner of a store, but most just honked their horns in a hideous song of idiots.

Two trips later, I found myself in the Bowery and stopped for a tall black man in a dusty black hat, with a beagle in his coat, so I knew it wasn't *Chester the Gimp*. Two cabs in front of me passed him by, probably because he looked penniless. He must have seen my guard was up, and offered kind assurance.

"Don't worry, I'm going to surprise you." He pulled out a wad of one dollar bills and asked me to drive up and down the street while he got out and gave a dollar to each homeless person he saw, then he saved a few for me. Everybody seemed to know him. He left with a tip of his hat. This world has a pocket of gems. Jerome wasn't around to tell, but would have raised an imaginary glass. I saw it in my mind.

I told my recent stories to the tribe, and learned that Rico broke his record getting from LaGuardia to Times Square. He clarified that he only sped on certain occasions, and I wondered if Richard had a strange effect on Rico's urgency, like he started measuring something he never noticed before. Richard said he got a stock tip from a fare and vowed to start looking toward the future for the first time in his life. He also found a new lover, and was considering acting school. Marcos was improving his English at an astonishing rate, and got a second job teaching Argentine Tango. We were shocked and so was he. He thought he had no talent, but when he went to take a lesson, women loved his calm, sweet guidance, and wanted him as their teacher. Emmanuel had another baby on the way, hoping for a girl. He was happier than ever, and didn't think of another job. He might still be driving. I was saving money to press on to Europe.

Jerome hadn't been around for quite a while. We assumed his mother had passed, but I wondered if all that was metaphor. We missed him, missed his mysterious wisdom, but kept the gift of his nature, regretting we never exchanged phone numbers.

I got pretty good at left-footed braking, backward U-turns, and made peace using the horn to survive. On freeways in L.A., you could be shot for using your horn. No kidding. In California, the art was to drive as fast as possible about three feet between cars. You've got to know your territory. I still think of the man down on Broadway, can't shake the image, never will.

Heading east one evening in midtown, I stopped for a huge full moon. It was rising right in front of me, orange between the buildings, hailing me from the end of the block, and for a little while, there were no other cars around. The city stopped and disappeared, leaving me right there in the road, thinking I could touch the moon.

Inheritance

By the time I was eight, I'd come to know of a cigar box my father kept in our garage, filled to the top with various nuts and bolts, washers, grommets, and screws. He inherited it from his father, but it always seemed to be a container for emotions I wasn't supposed to explore. It was an odd feeling, since it was easy to be fascinated with the metal offerings.

Dad was rarely an obscure guy, quite the contrary, but when he came near the box, he'd mention in some offhand way his father's stinginess of spirit. He recalled his father had an easy smile for others, but not for him. Strictness prevailed when his dad was around, as if glee or lightness should not be part of childhood, a fate he made sure not to pass on to my sister and me. I'm grateful for his clarity about that.

His habit, when near the box, was to straighten his spine, get close to being choked up, hide it with a pretend cough, then dump the box out on the garage floor and delve into the mess after a mysterious pause. He didn't elaborate, in words at least, even though he was a man of words, a born master of ceremonies, a journalist, a great public speaker who would quietly fold his handkerchief and put it in his top drawer, satisfied that he'd spoken well.

As if to express a variation of his father's teachings—that a person should regard possessions as if they might vanish any moment—my father made a point of declaring everything he owned to be a treasure; an old pen that didn't write anymore was something he couldn't throw out, owing to its treasure status. Of course, all items in the box were treasures, even the worn-out springs of rusted patio furniture. In time, I considered the dumping of the entire contents of the box to be an artistic moment, and grew curious as to how the metal fittings would spin and roll, bounce and spread, never the same way, over a six-foot swath. I also saw he didn't treat everything like treasures. It was more complicated; more like people had to be a mirror for how he needed the world to be, or how he needed to be seen, then everything was peachy. He wanted neighbors to be his friend, and they were. He was genuinely curious about hundreds of topics, so he interviewed people constantly, but his largeness of presence guaranteed that only a few would interview him back. It was as if he made them feel more real than they felt the moment before, and it made him feel impactful.

I suppose it bothered him how clearly I saw myself as part of a family drama when I was only eight. My punishment for seeing was to have to pick up the contents of the cigar box, no matter how long it took. He'd find the piece he was after, put it to use, and leave me to put it all away. That was the deal. He could be incredibly gentle too, loving and open, but not around that box. When I was thirteen I concluded there was something unfinished for him in all this. I invented a scene in which his own father dumped the box when my dad was a lad in Long Island, or a freezing morning in Chicago. I was caught in some odd repetition.

When I was twenty I forgave him for everything except making my very private mother wear a big Mexican hat on her birthday

in front of a blaring mariachi band. He knew how much she hated attention. When I was thirty I respected him. At forty I loved him more. When I was sixty, I took the box as mine. Now he's gone. My province became his swath; a mix of odds and ends on the cold cement when I need a part for myself. I have a daughter and son now, and never asked them to put away the pieces. I'm sure I carried on some other version of the scheme. They're off on their own adventures now.

I'm going to tell my children everything I know about the box. I swear there's good stuff in there, useful pieces that hold things together. They can figure out if they want to split the contents, or pass them to an unknown home. I've even got a new granddaughter who will likely be fascinated with the various parts when she's old enough to use them, maybe make it an art project. Fixing isn't everything.

Really, it's only a matter of minutes to gather up microscopic cotter pins and finishing nails, washers as thick as silver dollars, and a thousand bolts that don't have a better home. On a cold fall morning, it occurred to me the box was part of my inheritance. My God, it's really that simple.

The MG: Early Years

On the evening of November 9th, 1963, my father came home driving a 1958 white convertible MGA, a stunner with elegant lines, assembled in Abingdon, England, fitted with a left-side steering wheel. When it came into my life, I was a study in fluid motion, spilling over with anxieties that ranged from being sucked into a random sinkhole, to the terror of the mad dog that chased me down Fourth Street on unpredictable days. Funny thing, the dog would usually sit quietly on the porch when I rode my bike from school, but once in a while he'd bolt after me with unmistakable rage. Usually he got my tennis shoe or my book bag and held on as long as he could while I was going full speed. One time he bit my calf and I managed to kick him off and escape. But I never escaped the memory, or the fact that the attacks were getting more aggressive.

I tried putting reason to it, to soothe myself with theories. My logical mind favored the idea that the dog went nuts only when I wore a certain shirt or jeans that bothered his mind. My visceral theory was probably more accurate; that the dog could sense my fear. It got me to thinking that if I mastered the art of not showing fear, he wouldn't go after me. I saw a documentary that showed how predators can easily sense the fragile beast in the herd and you know what happens next. I never tested any of my theories and simply took a long detour home from that moment on. I also began to wonder if becoming a psychologist might be a way to nourish my endless perplexities and do some good along the way.

When dad brought the MG home, he glided around the corner just a few inches off the ground. It was an eye-catcher. The timing was puzzling. He'd been talking about wanting a sports car, but it always sounded like a passing whim. His story was simply that he spotted one in the classifieds and rolled the dice, but I always figured my sister and I were part of the reason he bought it when he did; you know, when your children enter the teen years and start rolling their eyes when you have something meaningful to say. They stop coming to you for the usual dad wisdom, but expect you to remain the anchor. I get it. You want something just for you. I went through it with my own children; amazed at the way we all came out the other side. Now they're strong, complicated adults with undercurrents of their own. The MG proved to be a bridge across generations. It only had one previous owner, a nurse who grew tired of keeping it running. For my dad, the task of keeping it running was the whole point. He bought a proper racing cap and loved to honk the horn to the children in the neighborhood.

Suddenly he was a scholar of books on the MG. I got to learn its secrets too, like how to put oil in the carburetor pots, take care of the fouled spark plugs, and clean the chrome until my eager eyes gleamed back at me. It was a variation of lust. Of course dad knew I was angling to drive it in just a few years. He reminded me he bought his first car when he was in high school, a model T, for $24 that he earned himself. There was no cure for that hunger except to feed it. Of course I'd clean up the inevitable oil leaks and sit in the car when he wasn't around, pretending I was driving to the beach with an imaginary girlfriend.

Although he was a retired Marine Corps pilot, he rarely swore up a storm in front of the family except when changing the oil filter on the MG. The Brits must have hated large-handed people, since he cut himself every time he changed the filter. I did too when I took over the task. As for the two six-volt batteries, we had to constantly get the hydrometer out, put fresh distilled water in the cells and charge the batteries overnight. If he didn't drive it for four or five days, the battery would lose its juice. None of the tedious things mattered since the car itself was juice. Fixing it became a source of confidence for me. There was nothing abstract about it. When dad didn't have time to charge the battery in the garage, he'd have me push it down the street while he popped the clutch in second gear to bring it back to life. We'd drive around to charge the batteries, but his real goal was to have a conversation with the wind.

We changed out the moon-shaped hubcaps—just too weird— even for the sixties. He put new mirrors over the wheel wells and refused to gussy it up with fancy wire wheels. Then he took it to a tuck-and-roll shop and got the seats re-done in candy-apple red leather. Finally he got a full engine overhaul and the sound was something so pure, he'd listen to it with his eyes closed before shutting it off, just to hear it purr.

My sister was two years older and got to drive it before I did. I appreciated her for not rubbing it in. She could have tortured meby dangling the keys in my face or reminding me I was way too short to drive anyway, but she wasn't a mean person at heart. Still, I'd have to be super nice and act older than my goofy self to ride with her, since what sixteen-year-old girl wants to be seen with her little turd brother unless he keeps a low profile? She'd zoom off to high school or her job as a swim instructor. Mom loved it less, but still put on a fancy scarf and would go out on the town in the MG. She wore the coolest sunglasses. To see them coming down the street, they were suddenly a European couple from a movie.

Mom wasn't keen on having to pump the brakes when they were spongy, so she rarely drove it herself. She was afraid of an accident, the sheer vulnerability of a tiny car among trucks and gigantic floaters like Cadillacs and Oldsmobiles. Sure enough, one time a pick-up truck failed to stop and came up over the back of the MG and nearly took my dad's head off. Privately, he told me it was a very, very close call. Mom was a reader, a student of crossword puzzles and handwriting analysis, wise in distant observations, smoking her Salem cigarettes.

By the time I turned sixteen, I'd grown half a foot and had taken the car a few spins with dad onboard. When I'd grind the transmission it made a sound so horrible I wanted to disappear, but he was benevolent, figuring it was part of the learning curve. Downshifting was tricky, but I was determined. My graduation test was to rock the car on our sloped driveway, showing I'd mastered the art of not lurching, not burning rubber, and not stalling out. I had to go up and down the driveway a few inches at first, then a few feet, without touching the brakes. He made me do it until he was satisfied. Finally he said I could take it around the block.

I was moving but the world stood still, with one hand on the steering wheel, one on the gearshift. I was smart enough not to speed. If a car has memories, the MG never told. Everyone touched its body in a different place, a different way: an open hand for the grill, a caress of the contours, a grip of the black steering wheel. By my senior year in high school, I was allowed to leave my skateboard or bike at home and drive it to school once in a while. I loved jumping out of it without opening the door, sort of *James Bond*

I thought, practicing my smooth. I was the only kid at school to have doors without handles on the outside. My friends were getting their first cars too. Barney Jackson had a 1949 Chrysler that could fit half the swim team in it. It was a thing a beauty but kept breaking down. It broke down seven times in the first six months he had it, and he had tears in his eyes when it threw a rod and he finally had to give it up. Evelyn Estancia got her grandmother's Rambler station wagon and put a sign in the window that said, "Don't laugh or I'll kill you. I mean it!" Steve Peterson hit the big time getting a 1955 Chevy, gray as a rain cloud, rusting, but it had the sweetest lines, and a sure, persistent engine.

Most parents in 1968 were sensible, and either didn't get a car for their kids in high school or couldn't afford one, but would sometimes let their child drive the family car. The exceptions were

The glorious feel of a first car, a 1949 Chrysler.

Starla Magnetti, who got a Mustang from some rich uncle, or so she said, and Roberto Hernandez, track star, who had access to all kinds of cars since his father fixed them for a living. He got a Corvette that was only a few years old. Roberto didn't gloat over it, but let it be known that nobody could beat him in a quarter mile race. He was one of those persons with natural, enviable confidence, and of course he was right about his car, so nobody challenged him. He'd screech out of the parking lot, putting on quite a show. We were impressed as hell, but it wasn't cool to suck up to him. Some folks were simply royalty.

Having a car meant you could get some privacy; suddenly you had a place to make out if you had a sweetheart, or you could skip class to go out for fast food. Making up credible lies to take a car out was part of the deal. Rome was burning, and we were Rome. Still, you can't blame a car as the reason to explore the world. We were seniors, looking for pranks before graduating. Steve Peterson asked a rather familiar question.

"Cooper, that's a cool looking car, but how fast will it go?

"My dad will kill me if I wreck his car, so I haven't tried for serious speed. Plus, I don't want to die young, regardless of my dad."

"I got my Chevy up to 97 mph on the back roads last week. I was scared and excited at the same time. The moon was barely out so my headlights had to slice a path through the ink of night. Good thing the road was straight. I hit an owl and nearly lost control. It scared the crap out of me. My heart pounded; everything flowed like lava. I was alone with all that wildness inside."

Steve was one of those rare persons who knew he wanted to be a literature professor by the time he was ten.

"Yeah, well your car is heavy. I'm afraid if I push the MG on those back roads, a dirt clod or a pothole would send my little car in the air and I'd tumble twelve times and die a senseless hideous death. Don't get me wrong; part of me wants to find out how fast it will go. Sorry to hear about the owl. I hope it was a sudden death."

"Oh, it was, it was. On a related subject, the watermelons are ripe out by Irvine just now and my brother's friend Stan just got a beat-up Dodge truck and wants to go out at night to grab some. We used to steal strawberries, cantaloupe, and grapefruit out that way. There aren't any streetlights. You can turn off your car lights and hear coyotes, see a million stars. You can tell your parents we're having a sleepover poker party before graduation. Want to come? Kevin and his dumb friend Greg are coming. It'll be fun. I think you know them."

"Why do you call Greg dumb?" I asked, already thinking like the psychologist I'd become. I was the only one in my crowd who would ask a question like that, since I found everybody interesting, even people who ignored me.

"Well, the only words I've ever heard Greg say are, '*Hell yeah, dude, let's go for it,*' no matter what the subject happens to be. Plus, he never changes his t-shirt. I mean never, so you know in a sin-gular way when he's anywhere near. He says he wants a girlfriend, but doesn't put it together with hygiene or any thought as to what might appeal to a girl."

"Maybe nobody explained it to him or tried to tell him the basics."

"You could be right. I'm sorry; he might be smarter than the rest of us. He just stopped going to school a while back and never said why. He's affable, that's for sure."

"Maybe there's something a little bit wrong with him. I mean, what if someone asked him to swim across the Newport Harbor at midnight, after drinking a bunch of beer? Sometimes people shoot a seal or sea lion just for fun between the jetties. Or what if you convinced him to go out to the end of the airport runway and light some bottle rockets?"

"Well, Greg would do it of course, no hesitation, but what's wrong with that?" said Steve. "It's not like you've asked him to kill someone."

I looked at him sideways, pondering the many kinds of dumb, especially my own pitiful failure to think of consequences. Finally, I circled around to the private thought that I wasn't very smart myself. I was the one who did the famous midnight swim in Newport Harbor with my buddy Barney, from one side of the jetty to the other, wearing dark water polo caps that made us look just like seals when we came up for air. And my friend Charles actually did the bottle rocket stunt, right near the airport. And he was a math genius, so you couldn't explain it by logic or some kind of science experiment. I mean, it was his idea, not that he meant any harm. None of us meant any harm, not even when we put up a weather balloon filled with helium trailing a roadside flare on a string. The morning newspaper said there were phone calls about a UFO. What a kick!

I realized I wasn't going to impress Steve with my artful job of toilet-papering Cynthia Pierce's house the week before. Way too common, unoriginal. Time to leave kid stuff behind. I told him that I was keen on Cynthia and thought I could win her over by a bit of artistry, imagining she would see that my stylized doodles in English class were the same as the lines I made in her trees with toilet paper. Instead, her dad heard something outside and chased me down the street with a shovel. Good thing he was overweight. I sprained my ankle but still got away. From a safe distance I saw him take a hose to my art, ruining the lace-like elegance. Tragically, Cynthia couldn't see my artistry the next morning, only the shreds of my world, and I couldn't let her know I did it, not then. Somebody else took her to the school dance. No, I wasn't terribly bright.

Fortunately, Steve was a guy I could talk with about failures and impulses, and he offered the observation that we had an easier time doing physically risky things than having a real conversation with a girl we liked. He said girls do it too, but in different ways, like getting all dressed up and hanging around you, but turn away the second you look their way. In his view, older people aren't much different; they get married, settle into jobs, have children, and act out a script they rarely think about, while not really knowing each other. All the while they keep private about the central matters that trouble them. He said his parents were a case in point.

"Man, you're dark sometimes," I told him, "but I can't argue with it. Maybe there's no such thing as childhood, just variations on a theme. Maybe the main thing is to stay out of jail and stay around people who seem good for you."

I cemented the insight by asking Steve if he had other, more personal motives for the watermelon proposition. Future psychologists can be massively irritating that way; always assuming one motive is a mask for another, when it's rarely that simple. Plus, it gives the false impression you know something when you don't.

"Give a person time and they'll find a way to speak about hard things, even the unspeakable. When I was six I remember my friend Craig told me during a game of marbles that the big marble wants to crush the little ones. He said the little ones always try to hide behind each other, but the one in front always gets hit the hardest. He called the big marble *father marble* in an oddly natural way."

Steve thought about my question of motives but couldn't summon other motives for his venture.

"This one may defy literary symbolism," he said, "it's all about stealing watermelons, eating some, and finding cool ways to splatter the others against telephone poles and street signs."

I decided I'd been too cerebral in examining the reasons anyone does anything. The key ingredient was to include myself in the inquiry. Such is the clash of private curiosity with the powerful pull of peers. I came up with a rescue plan.

"OK, I'll go, but what if Greg wants to stand up in the truck going 80 mph and throw a massive watermelon at an oncoming car. I mean he would think it was a great idea at first, and he'd do it to impress you guys. But he wouldn't think it through. It wouldn't occur to him he'd kill someone. Even a water balloon can be dangerous at high speed. We'll have to explain to him our targets are only structures, that it's enough to figure the timing of the launch, the angle of release. I guess I could go for that."

"Cooper, clearly we need a mastermind like you. The voice of reason."

"Wait, I'm not a mastermind or the voice of reason. I'm just saying I'd like to give it a try."

When the moment came, four of us were bouncing around in the back of Stan's pickup. He was frightening to a bunch of straight suburban kids: chain smoking, foul-mouthed for no clear reason, blaring country music, with long greasy hair blowing around the cabin. He'd be the kind to pick a fight if he was in a bad mood. We never had proper introductions to Stan, and he didn't seem to care who we were as long as we were cohorts. Stan left us off in the fields to get the watermelons, then circled back to pick us up with the lights off. He didn't want his truck to attract attention at the side of the road. Soon we had eight watermelons, ten-to-fifteen pounders. Stan pointed to one and kept it for himself, something like a commission for using his truck. Then, he got down to business.

"OK, here's the deal, I'm going to crank this baby up and you know what to do."

Oddly, we did. The first toss was Steve's. He could have been a physics' major the way he aimed his release at an old wooden sawhorse. The thud, the splitting sound, the crack in the universe, fascinated us. The sawhorse flew gloriously into a ditch; every detail was art in motion. We howled, yelled at the night, gave praise, and I remember falling to the floor of the bed of the truck, laughing at the purity of it all. Greg made a couple of tosses next, making glancing contact with a tree, scoring points for accuracy. Man that kid was a seeker, living in the moment, all about action, crushing the point of thought. He grabbed another watermelon and just threw it over his head, seeing how high it went before it liquefied in the middle of the road. We applauded in unison.

I threw the next two: one at a road sign reminding you of the 40 mph speed limit. I wasn't going to destroy a stop sign, that's where I drew the line. I remember the small disappointment of missing the sign, but was rescued by the laughter of others, who noted the melon sprayed across the dirt shoulder of the road like an asteroid kicking up dust. Steve likened it to his three-hundred-pound uncle doing a cannonball in the pool. I thought about the scene at first light of morning, when crows and flies would have a feast. People would drive by saying today's young people are wasteful. They were far superior; when they stole food, they ate every bit of it. I don't believe it.

My second shot won the crowd over; a dead center hit on a telephone pole that didn't budge. It was the splatter of the night. The howls lasted a full minute. For a moment, we were not human. I even got a nod from Stan; a little recognition from a wild man does something to a kid's mind, and I pondered the other things Stan did for fun, figuring his path might easily lead to stealing cars or worse. One of our group said Stan kept a gun in the glove box just in case of trouble. Something in my guts told me not to go with them next time.

College called, and I was game. All the parties, the access to alcohol, the sexual energy, people from other cultures, swept me right along. The MGA was with my dad or sister those first two years. Freshmen generally didn't have cars on campus. By my junior year it was a different story. I lived on Balboa Island during the school year, back when students could afford little cottages as rental homes. There were so many crowds to hang out with, friends from the dorms, the swim team, friends of friends, and by then I had a girlfriend, smarter than I, headed straight for medical school. I broadened my career options to include journalism, psychology, brain science, and photography, since they're all about inquiries.

In summers I started to drive the MGA everywhere, down to San Clemente, where I was an ocean lifeguard. The actual rescues were life changing. Things turned serious. It occurred to me that the relationship I'd been neglecting was the one with myself.

I didn't see it coming—the need to speak to myself. Not until a friend shot himself and another student who used to live in my dorm committed suicide too, within a few months of each other. They were serious people, strong students, but we didn't see their desperation, their futility. If I looked carefully, I'd have seen that some of us were getting into serious trouble with alcohol and drugs, laughing too hard, failing in school, covering the need for a reckoning, fighting monsters we couldn't name. Who were we supposed to be in the world?

On a Saturday night when I was alone, I took a ride on the back roads with an aim to clear my head. I thought of the previous fears I'd stuffed, all the energy it took to act normal when I was just as confused as the next person.

Oddly, being a psychology major had little impact on my emotions until I joined a Gestalt group therapy class and had to improvise an obituary for my friend who shot himself. The energy released, the shared abyss, the presence of others, the honest helplessness of grief, rushed me from all sides.

The MGA in Winter, hungering for Spring.

In that moment, I remembered the time I stretched out on a bed after hyperventilating and held my breath for four minutes and six seconds. Nobody believed me except Erickson, who was practicing the same art. We had a code of honesty. He understood all about pushing, to the point of nearly drowning when he tried for a distance record underwater. He would have died if not for our swimming coach, who was also an ocean lifeguard. Coach gave him CPR and Erickson made a full recovery. Coach G was a hero to us all.

In that moment, I was boiling inside and decided it was time to see how fast the MGA could go. It was a two-lane road with no cars around, near the same fields where we once stole watermelons. The smooth purr of the engine at sixty was a steadfast familiar vibration. I went past memories, some chased me, tried to bite me, and I pushed it to seventy to get away. I could swear the engine spoke, releasing its heart to me, reminding me of its roadster roots. I thought of the suspension, the narrow rods of the steering system, and how the u-joint was churning just under the batteries, inches above the road. At seventy-five I yelled out an answer to the engine, not a word really, more a howl, to compliment the confusion.

At eighty, I could see my youth, my mother's face, my sister in the living room playing the violin. Now I was the chaser, back and forth in time, shaking, with fear of coming apart in new vibrations. The screws holding the windshield on were rattling. I sent a hand over the windshield to feel the open wind, and pushed it to eighty-five. Faces lost their earthly meaning, and I fell strangely silent. White car, dark road, and an open lane ahead of me. Rattles became louder than wind but I had to find what I came for, so I pushed the accelerator all the way.

It's been forty-five years since the speed-run, and the MG is still going strong. Dad gave it to me when he couldn't get in it anymore, and not one second before. I've been driving it ever since. It's in the shop at the moment, time for new brakes and fluids. The odometer broke two years ago and we never bothered fixing it. I take it to my psychology office on fine-weathered days. People can't help touching it in the parking lot. Who can blame them? When I drive it home, I'm only going fifty but I'm in another realm. When I get home, I hesitate before turning the engine off. I've wondered about making a scrapbook where I place hundreds of photos of friends in or on the car, from 1963 to 2018: lovers from my twenties, my wife and children waving through the decades, friends and partners taking spins around the block, my cool nephew when he was fourteen, wearing his euro-style cap, my two-year-old granddaughter standing in the seat with both hands on the wheel. She already has that look, as if the MG called her in the secret language.

I don't think I got smarter until much later, and even that's debatable. Certainly not in my twenties, when I took the MG to Mexico plenty of times: Tijuana, Ensenada, Mexicali. We'd smuggle big packs of fireworks in the vent hose under the hood. You know, right next to the heat of the engine. I drove it to the mountains for camping, the lousy parts of Los Angeles, out to explore old mines in the desert, and to at least forty beaches between the Mexican border and Santa Barbara. Sometimes, a third person would sit on the back hood and lean over to hold onto the windshield, wildly high on drugs or alcohol.

I'm not going to get mystical about it, but the MG has powers that I still don't know about. Someone stole the insignia from the boot, and I ordered a new one right away. Maybe out of respect for my dad, I never called it anything but The MG. I started asking different questions than those about speed. I came to value a gentle downshift, reliability, the challenges of starting it up on a winter morning, the sputtering waking, the heat coming off the engine, warming my feet that way since the heater motor broke.

I never bragged or thought I should. I never needed to try to push the beast harder or pondered who was the truer beast, myself or the car. I remember topping out at ninety-three mph on that country road, and putting the MG in neutral for a long silent glide to let the engine cool. When we stopped, I raised the bonnet at the side of the road to let it cool some more. Did you ever listen to an engine block cool on a country road with nobody around? You have to be as patient as the night, sheltered from past and future, grateful in the dust.

Foggy Day at Heisler Park

April made the beaches grey, so I cruised down Cliff Drive from Crescent Beach, past Shaw's Cove, and Diver's Cove, and was called, as if the gulls decreed, to the beauty of Heisler Park, with Picnic Beach below.

The scene was framed in fog, the sun a teasing host, the paths a treat of turns, merging and inviting. Off the paved path, I came to a bench with a stunning view. A plaque there reads: *In loving memory of Bob Hedden, beloved husband and father 1919–1985.* A second one too: *Forever in Love with Laguna, Andy Hedden, 1957–2012, with love from your family.* I imagined gulls circling the bench when it was installed, with a nod or a tip of wing. Something about the word *beloved* was aspirational, I thought. So few of us are simply beloved, but it says so there, in bronze, and who would challenge it, leaning back, legs stretched, with arms supporting a dreamy head.

A young Japanese couple strolled by, on honeymoon it seemed, stopping every fifty feet to take photos of each other along the low rail. Another couple, Italian, saw them taking turns and asked if they would like a photo together. They spoke in gestures and winsome smiles, and the moment was cemented. The camera went back in the Japanese man's pocket, and they continued, slower than before, until the woman reached in his jacket, perhaps for lip balm, but she paused, hoping to be caught in the trespass.

He captured her hand with his own, and leaned to her for a small kiss, then another, until they stopped walking, and for a moment, no one was close on the path. I was far away and quiet. It's a gift to notice from a distance.

The couple risked showing their love in public, stepping off the path to rest on the lush grass on a small slope. Her wide-brimmed hat came off to hide their faces from others, and under the hat, a longer kiss, a sleep, but not a sleep; a dream of each other, while the scene below was full of twos: two waves coming in together, twin rocks offshore, the silhouettes of two palms to the north. The sun made a brief appearance, but fog came back in earnest to guard their tender reaches under its mist of gray.

The minute I left the bench, it was occupied by an elderly man and a fragile woman. They seemed to be waiting for their favorite place. He wore a white baseball cap and a loose blue shirt, while her hat was a bouquet on a bonnet. They spoke for a little while, though I couldn't hear, then turned their heads to the sea for a set of waves or two. He pointed in excitement at a lone dolphin he spotted. She missed it, having cupped her eyes for the longest while. He set his arm behind her back on the bench, not actually touching her, but it was a touch of a certain kind. I was thinking of a fifty year marriage.

She kicked a bit of sand from her worn blue sandals, seeing her feet as a child might. A smile came over her. A sailboat headed by. Pelicans skimmed the water.

I smiled too, though I can't say why. Maybe it's the moment a person finds their childhood wonders, regardless of their age. Past the perfect grass at the Lawn Bowling Club, and sculptures in their honoring poses, the gazebo offers a paradise of a view. It was a small wedding party, fifteen or so. An older Asian woman led the bride to a tall nervous man waiting beside a minister, and beside him a young woman played a solo violin: *Afternoon of a Faun* was the piece. The people walking by, locals and tourists alike, were heavenly respectful, and fragments of the ceremony could be heard in soft alliance with the perfect greys of the day.

I caught only a few phrases from the minister: *"the rest of your lives,"* breached the sanctity of the gazebo, and the rare word *"cherish,"* sailed through, and *"it's only the power of your love that will make this so,"* brought tears to quite a few. The betrothed were mightily serious, and didn't smile during their vows. They said other words I couldn't hear. Then, of course, the kiss.

I leaned against the railing near the gazebo. It's made to look like wood. The likeness is strong, but it's not of wood, instead a molded concrete, well conceived, built to endure the elements, strong and smooth, with details in the grain, protecting the place of vows. The sun did not return to the park that day, so all the shadows rested.

I took a different path back to where I started, noticing other benches with plaques. Each in loving memory of someone. I sat for a while, and with only the tips of my fingers, touched the plaque in memory of Jean Montgomery Engomar, 1913-1985, inscribed *"A Pacific View For All Who Love Her."* I won't know her in another way. The benches were freshly painted, and I visited several others. The fog held court all day. In early April it can go either way, although just a mile inland, the sun was scorching the canyons.

In Case of Rapture

Limping from a turn of an ankle, I stumbled to a park bench before the advent of a swollen sea. The bench was carved by messages of hate, gouged and memorialized in pressure-treated fir. Declarations of faith were just as deeply made, so I couldn't tell who was more in need—haters, or believers.

Pain brought me to the grain in wood. I came face-to-face with a carving of a delicate feather and a small letter *V*. A scar you might say, if it wasn't so beautiful. A shuffling homeless woman claimed the other end of the bench, with a lunchbox in her lap. I was a brittle, sorry version of me, but she broke our silence.

"The *V* is me. How do you like the feather I carved?"

I said I loved the image, that she had a gift for sure. I was thinking of the bird's-eye view of the little park, with so much grief below, where most have nowhere else to go. I was looking at garbage everywhere, but V dismissed my glance, saying a single feather should be enough to make anyone pause and wonder, if they have any pause and wonder left in them.

She looks for feathers in mornings. She said possessions get in her way. When she finds a feather suitable for permanence, the whole world comes in view and she begins her solemn work on knees too old to feel. People can use the bench when she's finished. V puts the feathers back to where she found them. In case of rapture, she doesn't want to be the one to alter what has fallen.

"That's my life. I guess you could say I'm patient."

V didn't ask for food or money. She asked about my pain. She spent last night on a hard plastic chair in an ER just to get out of the cold, then carved the feather in our bench with the tip of a broken can opener. I was the first to see.

She took me to nearby benches to see her other carvings. V had a shuffle; I had a limp. She said I could steady myself on her shoulder, but I didn't want to add my burden to hers. Don't bother asking her story. I tried. She thought she heard a peregrine falcon overhead, then gathered her breath to make it to a bench beyond a sycamore, and asked me to leave her there.

"You're very kind," I said.

"You have a smiling sadness," she replied.

I've returned to thank her several times, and offer art supplies, hoping not to offend. Pain can make visions appear—and there is dignity to ponder. I haven't found her yet, and hope she's safe from cold. I walk her trail of feathers, imaging the wood that knows her careful hand.

The Four Corners of the World

In hospital room 2E, you've got four men in white-sheeted beds, the four corners of the world. Most nights you have the usual monks and mystics, poets and fools. But on rare nights like this, you have cosmology, the descendants of the Anemoi, Greek gods of the four winds. There's confidentiality to consider, so I'll call them Señor Pancreas, Crushed Hand, Dr. Abdomen and Col. Alzheimer. There's only a thin cloth curtain separating us, and even that is drawn back most of the time, so we overhear each other's medical consultations, every family intimacy, every apology and anxious laugh.

Things kicked up around midnight after doctors finished their rounds. Crushed Hand turned into a mountain man, thrashing through the forest in a haunted morphine dream. The winds can see each other's dreams; it has always been so. We saw him use his one good hand to tear a giant branch from an oak tree and club everything in his path. It wasn't just an IV stand. After that, he tossed huge boulders in the canyons, screaming all the while. We saw pillows fly, but his dream was the thing that mattered. No doubt about it, he was related to Boreas of the north wind. When Crushed

Hand woke, he looked around the room, saw his place among the other injured winds, and turned his TV on as loud as it would go. What a jerk, not letting the other winds sleep. None of us wanted to be trapped in a room without fresh air. It bothered us that Crushed Hand didn't give a crap about the sacred nod of recognition.

He'll probably get out of here and go out in the world making a big scene about his wound. All he does is bluster. If you meet him, you can bet he'll try to punish you for his suffering. If you live in his territory, you're already intimate with his moods. You have to be strong and find your own meaning for staying.

I saw it all from the east bed, inverted vase that I am. I assumed that Señor Pancreas must have come down the line from Zephyrus, god of the west wind. He's the complicated one among us, his namesake having lived in a cave in Thrace. He had a huge number of passions and relationships in his time. His memories visited his mind in pairs, to pay their solemn respects, one on each side of his bed. He kept turning his head to hear their tales and wishes.

Look how he responds to each one differently, with smiles and grimaces, nods and frowns, entertaining a constant parade of memories. If the descendant of a wind god passes from human form, heirs and confidants show up out of the vapors to carry the traditions. Nobody explains anything, they just know to come, especially the invisible ones. You don't see any angry bedside drama with the west wind. Instead you feel the air rustling and you know a visitation has occurred. Sensitive mortals know the wind language too, how we eventually die from our passions. Zephyrus himself had a famous tangle with Apollo, but you won't see the scars unless you come up close to Señor Pancreas.

He's contemplative; the only one among us who can muster a private smile in spite of horrendous pain. He spent the whole night with his arms folded over his narrow chest, staring at the ceiling, saying the word, *unbelievable*, over and over, like he was watching a pageant about his life, projected on the ceiling. Sometimes he'd whisper the word *Luciana*, and the other winds suspected a great love—one he'd kept secret all these centuries.

I'm Dr. Abdomen. From my east corner, I saw flickers of light on the edge of Señor Pancreas' movie, but I didn't have a good enough angle to watch it with him. Don't try to tell me I was just looking at random patterns of light coming through blinds in the storm. He paused to greet me, saying he hoped I was on the mend. He was my kind of guy, offering care as an overarching value, so we opened up a spice trade route all over again. I had to use my eyes to return good wishes since I had a tube from my nose to my gut that hurt like hell and words were agony to deliver. He was less interested in words anyway. You could tell he'd made a certain kind of peace about moving on.

I tell you this world is spilling in a stream of water. If I ever get out of here, I'll swim the spill to a stream until it finds a river, then I'll travel to every sea that spawns the breeze, and name them all as kin. Ocean currents are intimate with wind. In a glimpse of death, I saw my ancestor, Eurus, wind god of the East. I suppose it's why I'm drawn to thickened air. Down the hall the Six Compassions dwell, although their nametags say they're nurses. A blessing is due for them.

Col. Alzheimer was in the fourth bed, pushing ninety, black and wise. He had us all figured as gentlemen at a poker party, and was confused that nobody brought the cards and chips. He was astonished at how things keep getting lost or turning up.

"What is this tube? I didn't put it here. Well, maybe I did. How about that? What is this shoe doing here? Somebody left it on the floor, not me. It's not my shoe, is it? Well maybe it is. I'll call my son. He'll know."

He kept trying to get out of bed, and it set off an alarm every time. The staff sent one of the Compassions to guide him back to bed, time after time, until he finally fell asleep. They were trying to avoid the indignity of tying him to the bed. In his confusion, he'd stir up a little storm, but forget it in a hot blast. He had to be related to Notos, Greek god of the south wind. You know how transient that wind can be: a soothing breeze one moment, a savage rip through the crops the next. All things considered, Col. Alzheimer had the most forgivable attitude toward life's inevitable frustrations. I would have loved to play poker with him.

Too bad his diabetes was out of control. We didn't know if he had a real son at all, or wished it so from need. The thought made the other winds sad. I could have announced myself as his son and it would have comforted him. But winds try not to lie while they move over the surface of the world. I swear, he would have wandered down the street, charmed one person and frightened another, until someone helped him change direction. That's the kind of wind he was.

I had him figured in another cosmology after my last morphine shot for the night, as Jupiter, one of the great wanderers of the heavens. Now I'm talking like Col. Alzheimer. *Who put the universe here? I didn't do it, did I? What's this tube for? Who put these men in the four corners? I'm supposed to be in my office seeing psychotherapy patients.* In the morning, Col. Alzheimer didn't mention his son or try to get out of bed. He seemed defeated, wouldn't even touch his breakfast. After a while, one of the Compassions came to tell him his son was coming to take him home, and the news filled him like a new father in the maternity ward. I've never seen an old man turn young so quickly. The other winds were at his back. Even Crushed Hand stopped his blustering when Col. Alzheimer sat up straight and made his announcement.

"I have a son? Oh yes I do, and he's coming right here to this room."

Willing Branches

I was seven when it first occurred to me I was growing older like everyone else. I was looking down from an airplane window, scanning the Grand Canyon for its layered secrets. I felt minuscule, and of course I was, but it didn't frighten me so much as wake me. I looked at my hands and they were still mine. I touched the airplane window, as if to anchor myself to the difference between near and far.

In teen years, I was always in motion, running between points A and B. I would light fuses on fireworks before I knew much about their dangers. I even made some new variations of pinwheels. The important part is to find the center and nail it in a piece of solid wood, so when it spins, it doesn't wobble out of control. The sensible side of me made practical inventions, and I collected beautiful coins. My favorites were the walking liberty half-dollar and the seated liberty dime. I never understood the plainness of coins minted later.

In my twenties, I jumped from one boxcar to another on a moving train through the Nevada desert under a full moon. I fell in love with randomness, and tried to give it meaning. Jazz clubs called me in the late hours. I found I had kindness in me, and opened to a fondness for unlikely people. I could not have made them up in the turbulence. I had fear, and plenty of confusion. My efforts to love were a brew of mixed desires. So sweet, the discoveries — so painful, a few. I made enduring friends, but wasn't prepared for the abyss of loss until I was in it.

I asked what stream I wanted to swim, and began to study intensely. I studied as if lesser ideas were profound, then left books for a camera and a trumpet, but came to see I didn't have to exclude anything just because my muse moved on. When I returned to books, I had a more critical mind but also a touch of sad awareness. Knowledge felt relative, skewed by the wanting.

In my thirties I was superman, loving my wife and children. My career as a psychologist moved faster than the river. Every summer, I'd hold my breath a minute or more, gliding underwater in the current of the American River, six inches above the rocks and clay. I'd come up for air, then go down again. The river ran parallel to the other rivers in my mind.

I couldn't stop replaying a soliloquy from a man I saw ranting in a market in Aberdeen, Scotland. "Wake up," he kept shouting. There I was, the only person who stopped to listen to him suffer on the busy street. He was lamenting the waste of life, but there he was, alone and angry. What kind of paradox made me stop to listen? I thought I was already awake. There was also a grizzled fisherman I met in the Shetland Islands, who said he knew me when it couldn't possibly have been true. "Don't waste your life on land," he advised. Then he kept on drinking. I see his face in every gale.

The next two decades were the deepening kind. I was chased by a somber ghost, and had tantalizing visions of clarity. I found mysteries in the two-way street of time. My children grew up and went on their own adventures, while my wife and I took Cha Cha lessons. My work led to levels I wouldn't have guessed as a younger man. I found myself looking at my hands more often, and little lines appeared around the eyes that were never there before. My wife was with me all the way, and saw the same in herself. She has the same smile as always. The place where my dog used to sit, by the large window in the living room, still draws my eyes in the morning. I can easily see her in my mind and summon the silk of her coat. Something wonderful about a tall, not too bright, English Setter. She used to stare out the window like a statue, noticing every passing car and person as if everything in the universe was new.

I suppose I'm like the canyon now, layered and dense, maybe too serious, cut by rivers and winds, leaning toward a kiss of lemonade, dancing Salsa in the kitchen with my wife, on the cusp of sixty-five. The orange blossoms are in full bloom. When they're gone, the lemon blossoms come. The gardenias will have a second go, then the jasmine. There's a waxing crescent moon, but I'm back among the orange blossoms, eyes closed. I see white spiral heavens, little galaxies whose fragrance took millions of years to reach the moment of a single inward breath. The willing branches seem to know me. They grow when I'm not paying attention. Look, I'm seven again. What kind of magic is this?

About the Author

J.L. COOPER is an author and psychologist in Sacramento, California. His writing highlights the lyricism in everyday life, relational mysteries, and the elevation of subjective experience. He has received five literary awards in fiction, nonfiction, poetry, and essay, including the *Tupelo Quarterly Prose Open Prize*, TQ9, judged by Pulitzer winner Adam Johnson, and the Grand Prize in Poetry, *Crosswinds Poetry Journal*, 2018, judged by Pulitzer winner in criticism Lloyd Schwartz. His full-length book of poetry, *An Ocean Large Enough* (David Robert Books) is available on Amazon Books. His short stories, poetry and a craft piece have appeared or are forthcoming in numerous journals including *The Manhattan Review*, *The Comstock Review*, *New Millennium Writings*, *Oberon Poetry Magazine*, *StoryQuarterly*, *Cutthroat*, *Hippocampus*, *Leveler*, *The Tishman Review*, *3Elements Review*, *Structo*, and several other journals and anthologies. His website is: jlcooper.net.

Also by J.L. Cooper

Available through Amazon, Barnes & Noble,
Book Depository, and most online book retailers.

Forthcoming from J.L. Cooper

Driving at Night in October
A poetry chapbook

A Perfect Stillness
Tales of Extraordinary Encounters

Spell of the Pelicans
A novella

PO Box #3092
Citrus Heights, CA 95611-3092
fivewarblers.wordpress.com